AN INVISIBLE WEB

Julie Coffin

Chivers Press • Thorndike Press
Bath, England   Waterville, Maine USA

This Large Print edition is published by Chivers Press, England, and by Thorndike Press, USA.

Published in 2003 in the U.K. by arrangement with the author.

Published in 2003 in the U.S. by arrangement with Julie Coffin.

U.K. Hardcover   ISBN 0–7540–8828–6 (Chivers Large Print)
U.K. Softcover   ISBN 0–7540–8829–4 (Camden Large Print)
U.S. Softcover   ISBN 0–7862–4875–0 (Nightingale Series Edition)

Copyright © Julie Coffin 1993

The text of this Large Print edition is unabridged.
Other aspects of the book may vary from the original edition.

Set in 16 pt. New Times Roman.

Printed in Great Britain on acid-free paper.

British Library Cataloguing in Publication Data available

Library of Congress Control Number: 2002111649

CHAPTER ONE

Even after all these years, the fear remained. And yet Lisa knew Marc could never find her. She had made quite sure of that. Her old way of life was gone, never to be repeated.

But still the fear persisted, today and every day, like an invisible web enmeshing her . . .

'Are you all right, my dear? You look a little fragile this morning. Not worried about the wedding, are you?'

Lisa glanced down at the diamonds on her finger, then smiled at the silver-haired man sitting beside her in the car.

'Worried, Fergus? Why should I be?' she asked brightly, but her eyes refused to meet his.

Fergus eased the car past the barrier and into his allotted parking bay, then silence surrounded them as he switched off the engine.

'After what happened last time, it wouldn't be surprising,' he suggested.

'All that was years ago!' Even to Lisa, the tone of her voice was unconvincing.

'This marriage won't be the same, I promise you,' he said softly.

'No marriage could be,' she replied, her hand unsteady as she undid the door and stepped out into the neon-lit basement of the

1

tower block.

Their footsteps echoed as they crossed to the lift, and the slam of another car door reverberating hollowly round the walls startled Lisa.

Fergus stopped suddenly.

'I've left some papers on the back seat. You go on up to the office, my dear. I'll be there in a couple of minutes.'

The lift doors yawned open; Lisa moved inside, turning to press the button for the seventh floor, but as they began to close, a hand reached out to stop them.

'Hang on!'

A tall figure twisted in through the rapidly-narrowing gap and she drew back, flattening herself against the side of the lift, her breathing quickening in panic. Smoke-grey eyes gazed down into hers and she could read their amusement as he spoke.

'I don't bite, you know,' and then his expression changed to concern as he studied her more intently. 'Hey, you're not going to faint, are you?'

Strong fingers gripped her elbows. At the touch, a myriad memories came rushing back, swamping her, overwhelming her with terror. The walls of the lift seemed to close in as she struggled to pull away.

'Let me go!' she cried, and her voice was shrill, her knuckles desperately beating against his chest.

His hand enfolded hers swiftly, stilling them.

'What's the matter? Are you ill?'

The lift shuddered to a halt, its doors sliding apart, and Lisa hurled herself into the corridor, taking him with her.

'Now will you tell me?' he insisted.

'I said, let go of me.'

'Not until I decide it's safe to do so,' he replied. 'You look as though you'll keel over any second. For goodness' sake, tell me what's wrong! Are you claustrophobic or something?'

In the safety of the office complex, her breathing evened out. She felt the tenseness lift from her body, and his grip eased.

'Well?' he persisted, his voice a mixture of concern and curiosity.

She lowered her eyes, unable to meet the sharp steel of his.

'I'm sorry.'

'I should think so, too! Anyone would think I was Jack the Ripper.' His humour had returned and she saw a cleft deepen in his chin as he smiled. 'I really do apologise if I scared you, leaping into the lift like that.' He regarded her steadily as he spoke. 'But your reaction was a bit over the top, wasn't it?'

Lisa's chin jutted.

'I've said I was sorry,' she snapped.

His lips pursed slightly.

'But you're not going to tell me what was wrong?'

3

The lift whined and its doors opened once more.

'Ah, there you are, dear,' Fergus declared, striding into the corridor. 'I see you've met Alex Miles. Can't remember whether I told you or not. Alex's here to bridge the gap while Tom James recovers from his hernia operation.'

Secure in her own office, Lisa felt the waves of embarrassment gradually recede. What sort of impression must I have created, she wondered. And of all people to choose, it would be the one filling in for the senior partner!

She sat down at her desk and began to sort through the post. There were a couple of new wills to be drawn up, a contract returned from signing, a power of attorney, letters from estate agents and preliminary enquiries for a new house purchase.

She skimmed through them, making notes on a tiny hand-held dictaphone, ready for her secretary to transcribe later in the morning, but she found concentration difficult as her mind still centred on that silly encounter in the lift.

He's probably decided I'm completely neurotic, she thought. Maybe I am. Marc made quite sure of that.

She glanced across the room into a small mirror, half-expecting to see the dark bruises and fiery weals that once had marred her reflection.

It's seven years, she told herself. All over and done with. Marc is safely behind bars. There's no way he can get to me now. No way he can find me.

A tap on the glass panel of her office door made her jump. When she called out, 'Come in,' it opened to admit Alex Miles.

As in the lift, his presence seemed to dominate the whole room and, studying him, she realised what a tall man he was. Tall, yet leanly built, and now that she wasn't so tense, she could appreciate that his looks were quite striking.

'We meet again, Miss Callington, but not with quite so much force, I hope.'

There was a teasing note in his voice that jarred on her. Why can't he forget the whole episode, she thought. Why keep harping on about it?

'At least you came in more quietly this time,' she replied, and when he continued to stand there, regarding her, she enquired tersely, 'Was there something you wanted?'

His smile deepened the cleft in his chin and Lisa found her eyes drawn to it, her mouth curving in response. It was impossible to resist. He shook his fair hair.

'I'm doing the rounds, introducing myself as the temporary new boy. Fergus was going to perform the honour, but he had to rush off down to the police station. One of his clients

5

has fallen foul of the law, I gather, so I'm having to brave it alone.'

He drew out a chair from the opposite side of her desk, and lowered his long frame into it.

'I've been browsing through the staff files hoping to learn a little about everyone,' he said, making a steeple of his fingers and resting his chin on them. 'You've been here for five years, I see. Did you come straight from university?'

Prickles of warning radiated through Lisa's body.

'No,' she said slowly, shaking her head. 'I left university during my first year.'

'And worked for a different legal practice?'

She saw his gaze fix upon her hands, and realised they were tightly gripping the edge of the desk. Quickly she hid them in her lap.

'No,' she said again. 'I . . . I lived abroad for a while, and when I returned to England, Fergus suggested I train here as a legal executive. I took a part-time course at the college of further education.'

'Good for you,' he said, leaning forward, and as he did, she recoiled, one hand rising in a defensive movement. 'You knew Fergus before you came here then?'

The back of the chair pressed into her spine.

'He's an old school friend of my father's. I've known him since I was a child.' She was aware of the tremble in her voice.

'What made you give up university? Did you find it all too much?'

Lisa hesitated before replying.

'I married.'

'Married!' His face registered surprise. 'I didn't realise you were married.' His tone sounded odd, almost disbelieving.

She saw his gaze move again to her hands.

'But you only wear an engagement ring.'

Lisa's fingers closed over it, twisting it round and round. Why does he have to keep asking questions, she thought. Why can't he go away?

The grey eyes met hers levelly, and she felt compelled to answer.

'I'm divorced. The marriage didn't work out.'

'But you still wear your engagement ring?' he persisted.

'I'm marrying again.'

His mouth turned down wryly at the corners.

'You've certainly led a very full life, Miss Callington. So when's the wedding?'

'Fergus and I are getting married next month.'

'Fergus and you?'

'Yes,' Lisa replied. She clenched her teeth.

'But he's . . .'

'Old enough to be my father?' she demanded, interrupting him. 'Is that what you're going to say?'

7

A steely glint came into Alex's eyes as she glared at him.

'Yes,' he agreed. 'That is roughly what I was going to say.'

'Then, Mr Miles, would you keep your cross-examination techniques for court and continue doing the rounds, so that I can get on with my work?'

His chair rasped across the floor as he rose to his feet and towered over her.

'My apologies, Miss Callington,' he said curtly. 'Please don't let me waste any more of your time.'

The small room vibrated as he closed the door.

How dare he interrogate me like that! Lisa fumed. The wretched man's only here on a temporary basis. If he does that to the rest of the staff, he'll raise a few backs. Just imagine having him on the opposing side in court.

But, she had to admit grudgingly to herself, he's probably very good at his job. In only a few minutes, he certainly found out a great deal about me—and I know precisely nothing about him . . .

Lisa usually ate lunch with Fergus at a little pub a couple of streets away from the office block. It was in an older, unspoiled part of the town, and retained its dark beams, low ceilings and small interjoining rooms.

At one o'clock, when she went to find him, Fergus's secretary said he hadn't yet returned

8

from the police station.

'Will you leave a note on his desk to tell him I've gone on ahead, please, Sally,' she asked. 'There's no point waiting. He might be ages.'

She smiled as she picked up her bag and headed for the lift. She was looking forward to seeing Fergus and quizzing him about Alex Miles.

To her relief the lift was empty, and when it stopped on the ground floor, she hurried out through the glass doors of the building into warm, spring sunshine.

A stream of slow-moving, lunch-time traffic blocked the road, and she waited patiently for a suitable gap before crossing. When she reached the opposite pavement, a rush of footsteps sounded behind her, accompanied by the frenzied beeping of horns, and a breathless voice said, 'Mind if I join you?'

Lisa's back stiffened.

'You are going to eat, aren't you?' Alex questioned.

Refusing to turn her head, she nodded.

'Then may I join you? You see, I don't even known the town, let alone where to eat.'

He sounded so pathetic that Lisa found herself smiling when she looked up at him. He grinned back at her, his grey eyes dancing with laughter.

'You're incorrigible!' she scolded, trying not to join his humour. 'I almost felt sorry for you.'

'But it's quite true,' he insisted, falling into

step beside her. 'I really haven't been here before.'

'So where do you come from?' Lisa enquired, determined to have the upper hand for once. 'I can't place your accent.'

'Originally, or last week?'

'Both,' she replied, declining to be sidetracked.

'Originally—Suffolk. Last week—Australia.'

'Holiday?' she asked.

'I only wish it had been. No, I've been working in Melbourne for the past seven or eight years. I went out to join my uncle's firm when I qualified.'

'So why come back?' she said, leading the way into the pub, through an arched door. 'Mind your head, the beams are pretty low.'

Alex paused to take in his surroundings, and she could tell from his expression that he approved.

'A traditional olde English inn—just the sort of place I've been missing,' he breathed, moving towards the bar. 'What will you have?'

'Apple juice, please. Anything stronger and I shall fall asleep when I'm drafting a particularly complicated will this afternoon.'

She moved to a small table by the bow-fronted window and sat down on a red, velvet-covered bench to wait until he joined her again.

'So why did you?' she repeated, taking the cool glass from him and sipping it.

10

'Come back?' he said. 'Oh, my uncle died. The other partner in the firm wasn't a man I got on with particularly well, so I decided it was time to return to my roots. Cheers!'

He took a long draught from his glass, then went on.

'Things have changed quite a bit over here. Jobs aren't easy to find any more, which is why I'm temping like this. Eventually I'd like to set up my own firm.' His gaze held hers for a long moment. 'How about joining me? You could act as adviser every time I go wrong.'

His eyes crinkled as he smiled.

'I dare say you'd be kept extremely busy. And I promise I wouldn't install any lifts.'

At that remark, Lisa picked up the menu, pretending to study it intently, although she knew its contents off by heart. Why was he bringing up that stupid incident in the lift again? He really was infuriating.

'Fergus and I usually have a Ploughman's Lunch or soup and a roll. Both are good,' she said. 'We eat at home in the evening.'

'Ah, yes, Fergus . . . I was forgetting.' Alex took the typed menu and read it through. 'Well, as this will be my one and only meal of the day, I shall plump for the steak and kidney pie.' His eyes narrowed slightly as he looked at her. 'You said we. Do you and Fergus live together?'

Sun shone in through the dusty panes of glass turning the diamonds on her finger into a

11

dazzle of rainbows. Lisa stared down at them, then with a swift movement twisted the ring out of sight into the folds of her skirt.

'I've lived with Fergus ever since I returned from France, but not in the way you mean. Zoe and I live there.'

Alex's eyebrows arched. 'Zoe?'

'My daughter.'

'Your daughter? But you only look like a child yourself.'

'I'm twenty-five,' she retorted indignantly. 'Zoe is nearly six.'

'I really can't keep up with this.' Alex sighed. 'Could you spell it out to me in words of one syllable, please? No, wait! If it's likely to be a long story, I'll go and order first. What's it to be? Soup or Ploughman's? Have you made up your mind?'

'Ploughman's. Oh, here's Fergus! You'd better wait and see what he wants as well.'

CHAPTER TWO

Trust Fergus to appear, just when Lisa's starting to unwind a little, Alex thought as he walked over to the bar. I've never seen a girl living on such a knife-edge before.

In the lift, she was almost bloodless with terror, and she flinches at the slightest movement. What's happened to produce such

12

an effect?

From the sound of it, she married very young. Was it because of the child? And the marriage couldn't have lasted long—she's worked here for five years.

Then there's Fergus. How does he fit into all this? Her father's school friend. That makes him around twice her age, at least. Even more so, from the look of him. Lives with him, too, but not in the way you mean, wasn't that how she put it?

So what's the attraction? Being a partner in a legal firm must make Fergus a pretty good catch, I suppose. But at his age, you'd expect him to be married already. Or is he divorced? And if he is, was Lisa the reason?

Alex leaned his back against the bar and studied them while he waited for the barman to appear. Not exactly the picture of a loving couple, he decided. They were not even sitting next to each other on that window-seat. Fergus didn't kiss her when he came in either. How on earth could he resist? In fact, they were almost business-like together.

'Yes, sir?' The barman took his order.

Maybe it's all for my benefit, Alex mused. An act they keep up while at work. But surely there should be some spark between them? A look? A gesture? A touch? Some hint of a closer relationship? Something that can't be hidden?

Lisa's an attractive girl, even if she does

13

twist that fantastic tawny hair up into such a severe knot. With it loose around her heart-shaped face, she'd look like a Rossetti painting.

Balancing the three glasses, he walked carefully back to the table. Even without his presence, he noticed, they sat discussing the client Fergus had been to see.

There's nothing between them at all, Alex decided. Nothing. So why on earth is she marrying him? The thought rankled.

'I shall be in court all afternoon, my dear,' Fergus was saying as Alex put the glasses on the table. 'And then I'll need to brief George Taylor ready for tomorrow. He's counsel for the defence in that stabbing case. Would you like me to leave you the car? I can take a taxi home.'

'No, don't do that, Fergus. You'll be late back. I'll walk, or catch the bus.' She glanced out of the window at the sunshine. 'It's a glorious day.'

Maybe I shouldn't have joined them, Alex reflected. Perhaps it's me that's putting them off.

He looked quickly round the pub and was aware that no-one else from the firm was there. Maybe this is their own little haven, away from the rest, and now I've barged in, spoiling an intimate lunch together. Well, there's not much I can do about it now, but next time . . .

His reverie was interrupted by the barman carrying their meals, and Alex saw Lisa recoil, her eyes widening in panic, as the man brushed her shoulder when he leaned over to put the plate in front of her.

The merest touch and it has that effect, Alex thought. But why?

*   *   *

By mid-afternoon the sunshine had changed to rain. It was more like April instead of the beginning of May, Lisa sighed, as she hurried towards the bus stop at five-thirty, and regretted declining the offer of Fergus's car. Raindrops misted her lashes and dripped from her hair on to her collar, chilling her neck as she stood, hunched against the rising wind.

When a car drew up beside the kerb, she didn't notice at first. It was only when the door opened, and a voice she recognised called her name, that she realised it was Alex Miles.

'Hop in before you drown!'

Momentarily, she hesitated, then as the rain increased into a deluge, she slid into the seat and pulled the door shut.

'You're soaked,' he accused. 'I did try to catch you before you left, but someone came through on the phone and by the time they'd finished, it was too late. How far away do you live?'

'Five minutes,' she replied, aware of the

uncomfortable dampness of her clothes now that she was in the warmth of the car. 'Turn left here. Then it's the second road on the right and up the hill.'

They continued the journey in silence, Alex peering out through the streaming windscreen to follow her directions. Once they'd left the town behind, the scenery changed to open countryside where large houses were set in spacious gardens.

'Next left,' Lisa instructed, and they entered a lane bordered by the lush green of rhododendron bushes. 'Last house on the right.'

Open gates led into a wide, paved forecourt. Alex stopped the car.

'Are you staying somewhere in the town?' Lisa asked, her fingers on the car door.

'I've rented a flat on the far side,' he replied. 'It's not exactly the Hilton, but I was lucky to find anywhere at all in this sort of area. It'll do until I move on again.'

Lisa remembered his words at lunchtime—
'. . . my one and only meal of the day,'—and found herself saying, 'Would you like to come in for something to eat?'

'Won't Fergus object? After a day of legal battles, the last thing I should imagine he wants is half the firm eating with him.'

'He phoned from George Taylor's chambers just as I was leaving. They're dining out—combining business with pleasure.'

16

'Even so . . .'

'His meal will only go to waste.'

'Well, if you're quite sure . . .'

The front door opened and a small girl appeared on the step, jumping up and down with excitement. And, as Alex watched, Lisa's face was suddenly transformed, a wide smile of delight changing it into an almost ethereal beauty.

'That's Zoe, my daughter,' she breathed, and her green eyes were luminous with love.

'Then we'd best not keep her waiting,' Alex replied, opening the car door.

The child hurled herself into Lisa's arms, then peeped shyly at Alex.

A miniature version of her mother, Alex thought, studying the tumble of red-gold hair that swung to the child's shoulders and surrounded her freckled little face.

'What's happened to Fergus?'

A rather severe-looking, grey-haired woman emerged from what Alex took to be the kitchen, and gave him an enquiring look.

'Oh, Moira, I'm sorry, I should have phoned, but I was rushing to catch the bus. He's eating out with George Taylor—a last-minute arrangement. This is Alex Miles who's filling in while Tom's recuperating. I've invited him to eat with us. Alex, this is Fergus's sister.'

It all grows more and more complex, Alex reflected, shaking the thin hand that gripped his. So Fergus's sister lived here as well!

17

'Mummy! Mummy! Come and see the picture I made at school today. We had all sorts of bits of things and stuck them on to paper and mine's a tree with a squirrel and a bird and lots of leaves. Come and see,' the little girl gabbled, tugging at Lisa's hand. 'You can see it, too, if you like,' she added, turning to Alex.

'I'm sorry,' Lisa apologised, giving him a rueful smile as they followed the child into the lounge. 'She's always a bit overwhelming like this when I come home.'

'I'm not surprised. You're obviously very close.'

Lisa's smile faded.

'Yes,' she said quietly. 'She means the whole world to me. You see, she's all I've got.'

And what about Fergus, Alex asked silently. The man you're going to marry . . .

An hour or so later, while Lisa was bathing Zoe, Alex went into the kitchen to help Moira with the washing-up.

'Oh, there's no need for that,' she scolded, as he picked up a cloth. 'I'm used to it. There's one of those new-fangled dishwashers over there, but I can't be doing with them. I like to see when a dish is clean. You go into the lounge and sit yourself down with the newspaper. Lisa will be back shortly.'

'No,' Alex insisted. 'You've very kindly given me a delicious meal. You must let me contribute in some way. I'd like to help.'

18

'Well, if you must,' she said.

'Have you lived here for long?' he enquired, watching her tie a flowered apron round her narrow waist.

'Only since Sheila died.'

'Sheila?' he queried.

'I'm forgetting you're new to the scene,' Moira said, plunging her hands into the sudsy water. 'Fergus's wife. She died last October. All very sudden, which was a mercy in one way. My brother was devastated. They were a devoted couple.'

Alex carefully lifted a glass bowl and began to dry it, mentally adding this new information to a rapidly-growing list.

'I can see you're wondering about the engagement,' Moira said, pausing for a moment to look at him. 'My brother's a very moral sort of man, you see. Old-fashioned in some ways. He insisted I came down here straight away. With Lisa living in the same house, I suppose he felt that people might get the wrong idea. Although I doubt if anyone would bother, in this day and age.'

And now he's marrying Lisa—is it pity or companionship, Alex wondered.

'I must admit I was rather surprised when they became engaged though,' Moira confided. 'Especially so soon after . . . well, Sheila has only been gone these past six months. But I suppose, bearing in mind what a life that poor girl has had, Fergus felt it would give her some security at last.'

'What sort of life has she had?' Alex asked, piling another clean plate on to the worktop. 'She told me she is divorced.'

Moira rested her wrists on the edge of the sink.

'Well, I don't know the whole story myself, only dribs and drabs. I'm not sure that even Fergus knows everything.' She delved into the water and produced a saucer.

'I hadn't met her then, but from what I gather, Lisa was quite a determined little minx when she was younger. You can tell that from the colour of her hair. Went off to university, met some young French fellow there, fell head over heels for him, and off they went to France to live. Oh, they were married by then, of course.'

Another saucer emerged from the suds and was vigorously scrubbed.

'Her parents weren't at all happy about the whole thing. She was only eighteen then, you see.'

'The marriage didn't work out?' Alex prompted, taking a handful of spoons and beginning to polish them dry.

Moira gave him a long hard look, her mouth thinning.

'That man turned out to be a vicious brute. Treated her abominably. Just shows what can happen if you rush into marriage without really knowing a person. He took drugs, drank

. . . never held down a proper job. He worked for his father, who had plenty of money. Dealt in property or something like that, the father did, over in France. Anyway, Lisa eventually returned to England—with the baby. I didn't see her, of course, but I heard all about it from Sheila and Fergus. Like a rake, she was, they said, and there's not a lot of her even now, is there?'

Alex heard the water gurgle from the sink, as Moira pulled out the plug and began to wipe a cloth over the draining-board.

'But why did Lisa come to live here? Wouldn't her parents have her back?'

Moira's thin hands squeezed the cloth dry and arranged it carefully over the edge of the sink.

'That was the most terrible part of it,' she said, untying the apron. 'Lisa's parents had gone out to France to bring her back. A couple of miles after leaving the ferry, their car was hit by a lorry. Killed them both outright.'

CHAPTER THREE

Lisa could hear the murmur of voices downstairs while she bathed Zoe, then read her a bedtime story. She wondered what Moira was saying to Alex. He's probably cross-examining her like he did me this morning.

21

Perhaps it's natural for him to do so. Perhaps that's what makes him such a good solicitor—and he must be good, she reasoned, or he wouldn't be taking over Tom James's work.

After she kissed her daughter good-night, Lisa hurried back to the lounge. The longer she left Alex alone with Moira, the more he was going to learn about her, and no way did she want that to happen. But, from the expression on his face when she appeared, she knew the damage was already done. His grey eyes were brimming with compassion. His welcoming smile seemed sad.

What has she told him? Lisa fumed, taking the cup of coffee Moira offered.

To her relief, Alex seemed determined to keep the conversation on a light level, recounting tales of his experiences in court while he was in Australia. When Fergus returned just before ten o'clock, it was to find them in fits of laughter over a dispute concerning the ownership of a boxing kangaroo.

'He didn't really produce the animal in court for the judge to see, did he?' Moira was asking, wiping her eyes.

Alex nodded solemnly. 'And the wretched creature started hitting out at the counsel for the prosecution. There was absolute uproar. People couldn't leave the courtroom fast enough. It certainly brought the case to a quick settlement and drummed up fantastic publicity for the kangaroo and its owner. There were queues half a mile long next time they gave a performance.'

The grandfather clock in the far corner of the lounge began to strike, and Alex rose to his feet.

'I hadn't realised it was so late,' he apologised.

'Don't go for a minute, Alex,' Fergus said, switching on the television. 'There should be something on the news about that Lincolnshire bank fraud. Might give us a precedent for that building society case Tom's dealing with . . . it'll be your case now.'

Half-watching the screen, Lisa began to gather up the empty coffee cups while Moira went to make fresh coffee for Fergus. A reporter was calmly relating the atrocities of a bombed city while smoke spiralled darkly behind him against a background of devastation. The picture reverted back to the studio where the newsreader continued listing the day's events. Lisa carried the tray into the kitchen.

'Leave that, dear,' Moira said, taking it from her. 'I'll do this. Fergus will want you to listen to that case as well.'

'It's not really the kind of thing I deal with,' Lisa told her.

'Never mind, it'll be useful to learn about, dear. You know how Fergus likes to talk over his work with you. He always says it helps him sort out everything clearly in his own mind. Off you go! Quickly, dear, or you'll miss it.'

It's Alex's case, Lisa thought ruefully as she went back into the lounge, and I certainly won't be discussing it with him.

The television was showing a scarlet car speeding along the edge of a sandy beach, leaving a rising trail of seaspray. It took her a moment to realise it was an advertisement and not part of the news. Alex, she noticed, was watching avidly.

Just the sort of vehicle I should imagine he'd like, she reflected, trying to remember what he'd driven her home in. It had been raining so hard that she hadn't been aware, except that there wasn't a great deal of room inside. She'd been conscious of Alex's nearness.

From the back of the room, she watched his fair head lean towards Fergus as he made some comment, laughter lines crinkling away to be lost in the smooth thickness of his hair. He always seems to be laughing, she mused, and as if sensing her thoughts, he turned, his grey eyes meeting and holding hers, enveloping her in their warmth.

'Come and sit down, Lisa,' Fergus said, patting the sofa beside him. 'You've missed the important bit, I'm afraid. It came on just before the adverts. I'll tell you about it later after Alex has gone.'

Alex rose swiftly to his feet again.

'Then I mustn't delay you. Thanks for the meal. I've really enjoyed the evening.' He held out his hand to Lisa.

It was if she were frozen, turned to ice, every atom of blood draining from her. All she could do was stare at the screen as if transfixed, her heartbeat drumming in her ears like the incessant throb of an engine.

The face filling the screen was gone now, replaced by that of the newsreader. She strained her ears to listen to his voice, every word searing into her.

'Marc Coursier, son of entrepreneur Pierre Coursier, was released from prison this morning after serving five years of a sentence for manslaughter. This infamous case will be remembered—'

Lisa heard no more. The room began to spin round and round, whirling her down into a vortex of echoing darkness.

A sharpness biting into her nostrils and throat forced her eyes open, her head jerking backwards from the pungent smell, her hand endeavouring to push it away.

'It's all right, Fergus, she's coming round.' Moira's voice sounded hollow in Lisa's ears. 'There now, dear. Feeling better? Take another deep breath of these smelling salts.'

Lisa shook her head weakly.

'Take it away,' she pleaded. 'Please, take it away.' She screwed her eyes tight to prevent the sting from penetrating further.

25

And then the full horror returned, the knowledge tearing through her like a vicious knife.

'Marc . . .'

'I know, my dear. I saw.' Fergus patted her hand gently. 'It had to happen one day, but five years seems a little on the light side to me. Don't you agree, Alex?'

'Right!' Lisa pulled herself into a sitting-position. 'Why didn't they keep him in for ever?'

'Lisa! Lisa!' Fergus soothed. 'Don't get yourself into such a state.'

'Marc's free,' she raged. 'Don't you understand what that means? You heard what he said at the trial. If I hadn't divorced him, he wouldn't have gone with that girl. It was all my fault, he kept saying, I'd suffer for it.' Her nails dug into the arm of the sofa, her knuckles bone white. 'And what about Zoe? Remember how he fought for custody of her at our divorce? Once he finds us, he'll take her from me, Fergus. That will be his revenge.'

Fergus looked up at his sister with distraught eyes.

'Do something, Moira. Please do something. I just don't know how to cope when she's like this.'

'Lisa!' Alex sank down on his heels beside her. 'This man has been in prison for five years. He'll have changed. He will have had time to regret everything he did to you. All

26

he'll want to do now is savour his freedom. Start a new life.'

Lisa's green eyes blazed back at him.

'You've no idea, have you?' she stormed. 'No idea at all! Marc is a fiend. A monster. I was married to him. I know exactly how his evil mind works. He has to dominate, to show his power. He enjoyed torturing me. It gave him pleasure. And now . . . he'll do anything he can think of to destroy me completely.'

'Moira! Phone the doctor,' Fergus ordered curtly. 'Can't you see she's hysterical? She needs medical attention, and quickly, too.'

'She needs your love and comfort, Fergus,' Alex told him, wishing he could put his own arms around her, hold her close, gently soothe away her fears. But if I did, he thought, remembering that episode in the lift, it would intensify her terror, and only succeed in making matters worse.

It was past midnight before Alex left and the house settled down for the night. The doctor, when he finally arrived, gave Lisa an injection. It was all he could do to calm her down and stop her fighting. Nothing anyone could say would ease her growing hysteria.

In the morning, when she woke, her head throbbed with tiredness. For a moment she lay still, watching motes of dust quiver in a sunbeam, remembering how, as a child, she believed her mother when she used to say it was fairies dancing. Her mother. A weight of guilt engulfed her. If it hadn't been for me . . . if I hadn't married Marc . . .

Marc!

Her body stiffened, her brain flooding with the memory of the previous evening. She could see his face on the television screen, staring out, as if looking for her.

It was a face she would never forget. Those clear, blue eyes above a thin, aristocratic, sculptured nose; that wide-lipped mouth; the long, dark hair that once had swept to his shoulders. It was a handsome face, revealing all his charm. A face any woman would be attracted to.

She closed her eyes, trying to shut out his image, but it remained, etched deeply inside her head, refusing to go away.

It was a miracle Zoe didn't resemble him. If she had . . . Lisa searched her soul. Would I still love her? And the answer came straight back without a moment's doubt. Of course, I would! She's my child, my flesh and blood, mine! There's nothing of Marc to taint her.

My whole life with Marc was filled with fear in some form or other, she recalled.

There was a gentle tap on her bedroom door and it opened to reveal a hesitant Moira, with a cup of tea in her hand.

'So you are awake, dear. I hoped you would be by now.'

Lisa dragged her tired body into a sitting position and accepted the cup, needing both hands to hold it steady.

'What's the time?' she asked, sipping gratefully to ease her dry mouth.

'Just gone two.'

'Two!'

Moira smiled. 'You needed the sleep, dear. Dr Colvin said to leave you as long as possible and when you woke, you were to take one of these.' She held out a bottle of small, white tablets.

Lisa eyed them, then shook her head.

'Oh, no,' she said. 'No way am I going to finish up on tranquillisers. All they do is keep me dopey.'

'Just until you settle down a little, dear,' Moira coaxed, shaking one on to her palm.

'I said no,' Lisa snapped, and tea slopped into the saucer and over the duvet at the force of her words.

'But, Lisa,' Moira pleaded, dabbing at the covers with her handkerchief.

Placing the cup down on her bedside cabinet, Lisa flung back the covers and stepped out of bed, swaying as her feet touched the floor.

'Oh, please, don't get up, Lisa. Dr Colvin said . . .'

'I don't care!' Lisa shouted, pushing her tawny hair away from her face with an impatient gesture. 'Where's Zoe?'

'At school. Where else would she be?'

'Have you warned the school?'

29

'Warned them?' Moira's voice was puzzled.

'That Marc may try to take her.'

'Oh, Lisa, now you really are being hysterical! How on earth do you expect Marc to even know where to find her?'

'Marc isn't stupid, Moira.'

'Well, he'd have to be extremely clever to locate you and Zoe, dear,' Moira said firmly. 'He doesn't know Fergus exists, let alone that you're both living here.'

Tension lifted slightly from Lisa's shoulders.

'I'm totally stupid, aren't I, Moira? You're right, of course. There is no way he can connect me with Fergus. No way at all.'

*　　　*　　　*

When the children erupted into the playground and out through the school gates, Lisa was waiting. Her body still felt strange and her head was throbbing. Moira had pleaded with her to stay at home and to let her fetch Zoe, as usual, but Lisa had refused to listen, and now she was waiting, with a curious feeling of unease and fear. Her eyes scanned the shrieking hordes. Zoe, where was Zoe?

As each child passed, her gaze turned to the next, and the next, and the next, until the last one had gone by.

Lisa's feet stumbled on the Tarmac, unable to move fast enough. At the entrance to the school, she paused. Where was Zoe's classroom? Left or right?

She forced her brain to remember. Reluctantly, it churned. The left. The right. Which way?

Class one. Mrs . . . I hear the name every day. Zoe never stops chattering about her. Mrs . . .

'Can I help you?'

A thin, grey-haired man appeared, regarding her through gold half-glasses. The headmaster, Lisa remembered, she'd seen him at the children's Christmas concert.

'My daughter,' she gasped, panic rising to snatch at her voice. 'My daughter. I can't find her.'

'Your daughter's name?'

'Zoe. Zoe Callington.' Not Coursier. She always refused to call her that.

'Zoe Callington,' he repeated. 'And her class?'

'One. The first class. She only started in September,' Lisa gabbled, unable to prevent the words from tumbling out.

'Zoe Callington. Class one. Mrs Tompkins. This way please, Mrs Callington.'

Obediently, she followed him along the shiny-floored corridor, passing rows of empty pegs, navy shoe bags hanging below them. Which one is Zoe's, she wondered.

There was a throat-catching smell of chalk and disinfectant. My school smelled the same,

31

she reflected. Do all schools?

At the end of the corridor, the headmaster stopped and opened a door. Eagerly, Lisa moved forward.

Ahead of her the room loomed. Knee-high tables and chairs were tidily arranged in groups. Pictures, full of colour, adorned every wall. A long window looked out on to a wide, green playing-field where goalposts stood at either end. Lisa took in every detail.

Then her gaze returned to the man standing next to her.

'I'm afraid, Mrs Callington, there's no-one here.'

CHAPTER FOUR

Ice slid down Lisa's spine and filtered into her body. What on earth could have happened to Zoe?

'She must be here. She has to be here,' she cried, striving to keep her voice steady.

'You're quite sure that no-one else has collected her?' the headmaster questioned. 'Was she having tea with another child perhaps? She may have forgotten to tell you.'

'Of course not!'

A twist of suspicion spiralled into Lisa's mind, increasing with every second.

Marc!

But how could he find Zoe? Her mind was racing. It's impossible for him to know where we're living now. No way at all.

Or is there?

A door banged somewhere in the school building. Footsteps echoed down the long corridor. Voices. One soft. One high and piping. Lisa's heart began to race, and she spun round, running towards the sound.

'Oh, Miss Callington, I'm so sorry,' Mrs Tompkins said, hurrying up, her plump face anguished. 'Were you getting worried? Zoe tripped and bumped her nose on the door as the children were rushing out. I'm afraid some of them do get a little reckless when it's going-home time.' She smiled down at the little girl. 'I've been mopping you up, haven't I?'

Lisa wasn't listening. Her arms lifted the child, hugging her tight, kissing her. She battled to choke back the tears that were threatening to fall.

'Mummy!' Zoe protested, wriggling free. 'Mind my nose! It might bleed again. All over you. It was lots and lots of really red blood, wasn't it, Mrs Tompkins? Really, really red. Why are you here? Where's Auntie Moira?'

Lisa felt weak with relief. If anything happened to Zoe, she thought, what would I do? Her face set into a picture of cold determination. But nothing's going to happen to Zoe, she told herself, I'll make sure of that for the rest of my life. No matter what it takes,

33

I will make sure she is safe.

Lisa hurried Zoe out to the playground, ignoring the little girl's questions as to why they were in such a hurry. Lisa just tightened her grasp on Zoe's hand as they headed for home.

*   *   *

'Why haven't I got a daddy?' Zoe asked, while Lisa was tucking her into bed that night. It had been a recurring question since the day her daughter started school, and one that Lisa dreaded.

'All the boys and girls in my class have daddies. Some have two daddies. They've got real daddies that live in different houses, and new daddies that live in their house.' Zoe's freckled face screwed into a thoughtful frown. 'That means they get two presents when it's their birthday. I don't get any presents.'

'Of course you get presents,' Lisa chided, smoothing the duvet around the little girl. 'And I've shown you that photograph of your daddy lots of times.'

Even though I hate seeing it, bringing back all those memories I'm trying so hard to forget, Lisa reflected.

'Why is it in a box in your bedroom?' Zoe said. 'Why can't it be on the mantelpiece with all the photographs of me?'

'Because . . . '

How can I tell my daughter that I don't want her to see her father's face? How can I explain that I never want to be reminded of the way I was bewitched by that face? Zoe couldn't understand that there was an evil streak behind those devastating looks.

'Because Uncle Fergus is going to be your daddy soon.'

'Uncle Fergus has white hair,' Zoe scorned. 'Daddies don't have white hair. Only grandpas do.' Her small mouth dropped. 'Why haven't I got a grandpa? And a grandma? All the boys and girls . . .'

'Zoe!' Lisa interrupted before her daughter could grow too mournful. 'Grandma and Grandpa Callington went to Heaven when you were a little baby. You know that very well.'

'Why did they go to Heaven?'

'Look, darling, it's way past your bedtime. You're only spinning it out.'

'If I had a daddy, he wouldn't make me go to bed at seven o'clock,' Zoe grumbled. 'Daddies let you stay up for hours and hours 'til nine past ten o'clock and sometimes 'til almost the next day. Hannah's new daddy lets her have a drink of beer at the pub.'

'Zoe!'

'He does! And she never has to go to bed 'til she wants to.'

'You're making up stories, Zoe,' Lisa scolded.

'I'm not making up stories,' Zoe protested,

35

her bottom lip thrusting forward. 'Hannah said so.'

The front door bell chimed, and Zoe sat up.

'That's visitors. Can I come downstairs and see them?'

'No,' Lisa declared, curious as to who it could be.

Fergus rarely invited guests. He was always far too busy reading up on some of his current work. If they did entertain, it was at the weekend. But even those occasions were infrequent.

She heard his step in the hall, and the noise of the door opening, followed by silence. Kissing Zoe good-night, she ran swiftly down the stairs.

'Just a letter, my dear,' he said, handing her a long, white envelope, and she saw puzzlement in his pale, blue eyes. 'Slipped through the box by hand.'

Her gaze took in the scrawled, black-inked words.

Lisa Coursier.

Her breath caught in her throat. No-one ever called her that.

Frantically, her fingers tore away the flap and tugged out a single sheet of paper. The message it contained was brief.

I shall have my child.

Her legs began to tremble as if unable to support her weight.

'Marc's out there, Fergus,' she whispered, her gaze still on the words. 'He's out there,

36

waiting, watching. He knows I'm in here, Fergus.'

'Pull yourself together,' Fergus ordered sharply, taking the letter from her. 'There's no need to get hysterical again. I'll phone the police straight away and ask them to send someone round here.'

He picked up the telephone receiver and, with his hand poised over the numbers, said, 'Go and find Moira, my dear. Ask her to make you a cup of tea.'

'Fergus! Listen to me! Marc's out there. You've no idea what he's like. He's clever. He's devious. Sending a policeman won't be any good. Even with a dozen policemen, it would be impossible to comb the whole neighbourhood.' Her voice rose higher. 'He could be anywhere by now. Even in the house. Is the back door locked? The windows?'

The front door bell suddenly shrilled again behind her, sending her rigid with terror. Fergus reached out to undo the catch.

'Don't!' she shrieked. 'Don't let him in.'

Slipping on the chain, Fergus opened the door cautiously, then with a sigh of relief, undid the chain again.

'Alex! Come on in. I've almost sorted out those documents for you. Sorry about the confusion. Bit of a panic at the moment.'

Alex stepped into the hall, aware of the atmosphere of tension. Moira hovered in the kitchen doorway. Fergus looked bewildered, and Lisa's face was bleached of colour, her eyes huge and staring.

'Did you see anyone out there?' she demanded, her fingers clutching at his sleeve.

He shook his head. 'Apart from a car turning the corner, the lane was deserted. Why? What's happened?'

'Can I come and see the visitors, Mummy?' Zoe stood halfway down the stairs, clutching a worn-looking teddy-bear. 'Just for a minute?' she wheedled.

'Take her back to bed, Lisa,' Fergus instructed. 'We don't want the child involved in all this pandemonium. Go on through to the lounge with Moira, Alex. I have to make a phone call. Nothing to worry about.'

At the words, Lisa threw him a scathing look, then, taking Zoe's hand, she led her back upstairs.

'What's up?' Alex asked Moira, seating himself in a chair by the window.

Moira shrugged her narrow shoulders and shook her head.

'I've no idea. Fergus and I were watching a wildlife programme on television when someone rang the bell, a couple of minutes before you arrived. He went to answer it, and there's been chaos ever since. A letter of some sort, from what I can gather. Whatever it was, it threw Lisa into a panic again. She worries me. Her nerves really are in a terrible state. I do hope Fergus realises what he's taking on.'

She pursed her thin lips.

Her brother came back into the room, his thin face smiling.

'Well, that's all right. They're sending someone round to check straight away.'

'Check what?' Alex enquired.

'There's been a letter from Lisa's ex-husband. Could be taken as a threat.' He passed the note to Alex, and then went over to pour a drink. 'Will you join me?' he asked, holding out a cut-glass decanter. 'I think we could all do with a stiff whisky.'

'Not for me,' Alex said. 'I'm driving.'

'Coffee then?' Moira asked, rising to her feet. 'I'm sure Lisa needs some.'

'Needs what?' Lisa questioned, entering the room and Alex noticed the pallor of her skin remained. Her green eyes were icy.

'Coffee, dear.'

Lisa brushed her hand across her forehead in a weary gesture.

'Thanks, Moira.' Her gaze caught the letter Alex was holding and he saw her expression tighten. 'Have you read it?'

He nodded.

'Marc means what he says, Alex. And he'll go all out until he succeeds. He's that sort of man.'

'There's nothing at all for you to worry about, my dear,' Fergus soothed. 'The police are on their way.'

'They won't find him,' she said flatly, sinking

39

into an armchair and drawing her knees up to her chin.

'They will at least scare him off, if he is hanging around the house,' Alex observed.

'If?' Lisa demanded shrilly, straightening up again. 'Don't you believe me either? I know he's out there somewhere.'

'Of course I believe you,' he replied, leaning towards her. 'But I very much doubt he'll stay around. With the mentality he has, having frightened you with the letter, he'll have had his satisfaction for today. Now he'll sit back and wait a while.'

Alex actually understands how Marc's mind works, Lisa thought, staring at him with a sense of relief.

'That's exactly what he'll do. He won't rush things. Slow and persistent torment is his way. Subtle. Long, drawn-out.'

Her face is a picture of agony, Alex thought. Now she's all eyes, and they reveal everything. How can Fergus be so impassive? Why doesn't he hold her close, soothe away her torment and fear?

For the third time that evening, the doorbell sounded, and everyone in the room froze, heads turning, until Fergus went to answer it.

Seeing Lisa, sitting there, taut as a wire, Alex stretched out his hand and placed it over her twisting fingers. Involuntarily, they jerked away as though stung.

'The garden and lane have been searched,'

Fergus announced, ushering in two uniformed men. 'And there was no sign of Coursier, or anyone else, you'll be relieved to know, my dear.'

'Did you expect to find him sitting patiently out there on the swing?' Lisa enquired bitterly.

Fergus frowned.

'Just show the sergeant the letter, Lisa. He'll need to take it away for fingerprinting.'

'There's no need,' she retorted. 'I can tell you who it's from.'

'We have to be certain, Miss Callington,' the sergeant said, studying the sheet of paper, then the envelope.

'It's from Marc,' she declared hotly. 'I recognise his writing.'

'When did you last see him?'

'At his trial—five years ago.'

'A long time.'

Lisa thrust out her chin defensively.

'I did live with my husband for almost two years before that.'

'And five years have passed since then, Miss Callington.'

'No-one else calls me Lisa Coursier,' she snapped.

'It is your name.'

'Was my name. After the divorce, I reverted to my maiden name, Callington, as you so rightly call me,' she added wearily.

'Well, I don't think you have any need to worry unduly, Miss Callington. The man—

whoever he might be—won't hang around the district. He's done what he had to—delivered the letter.'

The sergeant's cool gaze settled upon her. 'What you have not taken into account, Miss Callington, is that this letter could have been delivered by someone other than the writer.'

He turned on his heel and moved towards the door, followed by the second officer.

'Which is precisely why we wish to examine this envelope for fingerprints. Once we know who made the delivery, we shall be well on our way to discovering who wrote it.'

CHAPTER FIVE

'What the sergeant's trying to say,' Alex told Lisa gently after both policemen had gone, 'is that Marc Coursier might not be anywhere in the district. He could've paid someone else to do his dirty work.'

'But he still must know where I live,' she insisted. 'I can't understand it. After the divorce I put my parents' house on the market and moved right away from the area. When Fergus and Sheila found out what I was doing, they persuaded me to stay here with them. Sheila adored children, didn't she, Fergus? She regretted so much not having any.'

'We both regretted it,' Fergus murmured.

'Sheila suggested that I take a job, while she took care of Zoe.' Lisa glanced across at Fergus. 'I think she felt—you both felt—that after all that had happened, it would be a good thing for me to get out into the world again. If I hadn't . . . well, everything would have built up out of all proportion. She was a wonderful person. Always so considerate. And she adored Zoe, didn't she?'

Fergus nodded silently.

'Marc knew nothing of Sheila and Fergus. There was no reason why he should.' Lisa's voice hardened. 'He had no occasion to meet them. We didn't have a formal wedding with invited guests.' Lisa's fingers closed over her diamond ring for a brief moment, then relaxed. 'So how could he have discovered I was here?'

'It is a complete mystery,' Fergus agreed.

'When you became engaged, was there any announcement?' Alex asked. 'A notice in the local paper, or something like that?'

Lisa's eyes widened in dismay.

'*The Times*,' she said, 'and *The Telegraph*. You put an announcement in their Forthcoming Marriages column, didn't you, Fergus?' Her gaze spun back to Alex. 'But Marc was in prison then.'

'He probably read newspapers there. And didn't you say his father bought and sold properties in France and Britain?'

She nodded. 'Dilapidated ones. He

renovated them, then sold them at a fantastic profit. When we were first married, Marc and I toured France looking for old cottages and farmhouses. Pierre Coursier did the same over here. He would offer a ridiculous price to take the property off the owner's hands as he put it. He'd do a quick restoration job, as cheaply as he could and re-sell. That's why he's a multi-millionaire now.'

'*The Times* and *Telegraph* have excellent columns for advertising the sale of holiday properties,' Alex observed wryly.

'You mean Marc's father could have seen the announcement and told his son?' Fergus said.

'Exactly! Can you remember how the announcement was worded?'

'I can do better than that, I can show you,' Fergus replied.

He left the room for a moment and returned holding two small slips of newsprint, which he proceeded to read aloud.

'Mr F. C. McDonald and Miss L. A. Callington. The engagement is announced between Fergus, elder son of the late Major and Mrs Stewart McDonald of Hillford, Middlesex, and Lisa, only daughter of the late Mr and Mrs P. A. Callington of Norton, Suffolk.'

'It doesn't mention the fact that you both live here in Ferryham,' Alex pointed out.

'Ah,' Fergus said, looking troubled. 'The

44

same week the announcement appeared, I was in court. Rather a nasty mugging. One man was so badly beaten up, he suffered brain damage. It attracted a great deal of publicity from the media, both television and national Press. I presume you were still in Australia at the time and missed it. Each time I left court, I had a microphone or camera thrust into my face. My name was brought to the public's attention.'

'And Coursier or his father could have linked it with the engagement announcement,' Alex mused, frowning slightly. 'It's a bit of a remote chance.'

Fergus shrugged. 'It seems likely when you think about it.'

'Pierre Coursier hates me almost as much as Marc does,' Lisa put in. 'He blamed me for Marc ending up in prison.'

'Why did he go to prison?' Alex enquired, pushing aside some magazines so that Moira could place the coffee tray on a small table.

'Manslaughter,' Lisa said abruptly. 'A couple of days after our divorce, he met a girl and took her back to his hotel room. He was a little too violent, and she died from a fractured skull. He said he was drunk and pleaded extenuating circumstances.'

There was a slight creak as the lounge door widened, and everyone's head turned. Zoe stood there, trying in vain to button her dressing-gown which was inside out.

'Bruno Bear would like a biscuit,' she announced, producing the toy from under her arm.

'Would he now?' Lisa declared. 'Then he'll have to wait until tomorrow. If he has one now, he'll finish up with a tummy-ache.'

'I could eat some of it for him,' Zoe suggested, inching her way round the door, her wide eyes taking in the scene.

'Not at this time of night, you couldn't,' Lisa replied. 'Come on, back upstairs you go.'

Zoe ran quickly across the room and leaned on the arm of Alex's chair.

'Hello,' she said, beaming up at him. 'Have you come to see us again?'

'Zoe!' Lisa warned, as Alex hoisted her on to his knee.

'It's no use turning on the charm. You're going up to bed now.'

'I'm being polite, Mummy,' Zoe admonished, frowning at Lisa. 'You always say I should be polite when I meet people.'

'Not at eight o'clock at night when you're supposed to be fast asleep, young lady.'

'But I'm not fast asleep, Mummy. You were all making too much noise. Me'n Bruno tried and tried to go to sleep, but we couldn't.' She gave her mother a winning smile. 'We might if we had a biscuit though.'

'Oh, Zoe, I despair of you!' Lisa wailed.

'She's obviously inherited your legal talent, Lisa.' Alex laughed. 'The art of gentle

46

persuasion to win her case.'

'Does that mean I can have a biscuit?'

'Can she?' he pleaded.

Lisa sighed. 'Whose side are you on?'

Alex's grey eyes crinkled. 'Oh, the winning one every time.'

'You shouldn't encourage her, Alex,' Fergus remarked sternly, spooning sugar into his coffee. 'Zoe has to learn self-control.'

'At five years old?'

'Discipline should begin as soon as it can be understood. That's half the trouble today—and why our courts are overloaded.'

'Without crime, wouldn't you and I be out of a job?' Alex enquired drily.

'Zoe! Eat that biscuit quickly and go to bed,' Fergus commanded.

The child's mouth tightened into a small knot and Lisa felt a wave of unease. It was an expression that boded ill.

'You're not my daddy,' Zoe declared, her freckled cheeks beginning to glow with colour. 'Only daddies and mummies can say what to do. And teachers,' she added.

'You see what I mean?' Fergus thundered, glaring at Lisa. 'The child's becoming totally out of control. I will not have her interrupting my evening. Take her upstairs at once.'

'She's over-tired,' Moira soothed. 'Shall Auntie take you up to bed?'

Zoe's face scowled and she buried herself into the depths of Alex's arm.

47

'No!' she exclaimed.

Lisa closed her eyes, dreading what would come next. When Zoe decided to be stubborn, there was no shifting her. Any second now, a full-blown tantrum would erupt.

'Bruno's fallen asleep,' Alex said quietly, stroking the teddy's flattened nose. 'He really ought to be tucked up in bed, don't you think, Zoe?'

The little girl threw Alex a quick, suspicious look, and was met with solemn concern.

'Does he sleep in your bed with you?' Alex asked.

She nodded, giving the bear a puzzled glance.

'Then shall I carry him upstairs very carefully, so he doesn't wake up?'

Zoe nodded again, her gaze probing Alex's.

'Will you show me the way then? Perhaps you'd best stay with him just in case he wakes up again and misses you.'

Easing herself down from his knee, Zoe tiptoed towards the door, and tugged it open. Alex followed.

'Be very quiet,' she instructed him in a whisper.

So, Lisa thought wryly, not only is he brilliant with his cross-examination technique, but also with his powers of persuasion.

Trailing behind them, she went up the stairs and when she reached the top, there was Zoe tucking one corner of the duvet round her teddy-bear, before climbing into bed.

'Good-night, Zoe,' Alex said, blowing her kiss.

'Will you come and see me'n Bruno again tomorrow?' the little girl asked eagerly.

'One day, perhaps, if Uncle Fergus invites me.'

'I'm inviting you,' she protested. 'And Mummy will, won't you?'

Alex turned and Lisa's breath caught in her throat as laughter turned his eyes to the soft grey of summer clouds.

'Will you, Mummy?'

Lisa's chin tipped upwards. 'That's entirely up to Fergus,' she said, emphasising the final word. 'Has he given you the papers you need?'

'Yes,' Alex replied, his laughter dying. 'And as I seem to be outstaying my welcome, I'll go.'

'It's Bruno's birthday tomorrow.' Zoe's whisper interrupted the tension growing between them. 'He's having a party and you can come.'

Alex smiled, blew her another kiss, and went downstairs without another word. Minutes later, Lisa heard the front door shut.

*   *   *

An hour before the postman called next morning, there was an envelope lying on the mat. With shaking fingers, Lisa picked it up.

Lisa Coursier, she read, written in the same

49

black scrawl.

The note inside was longer this time.

Only two policemen? You'll need many, many more than that. And they'll never prevent me doing what I intend to do. Remember, Zoe is my child.

She was still standing there, powerless to move, when Fergus came down the stairs, pulling on the jacket of his suit.

'The post has arrived early this morning, my dear,' he commented, walking past her towards the kitchen.

Lisa made no reply.

'For you?' he enquired, looking back at her, and his expression changed. 'Is something wrong, my dear?'

Silently, she held out the sheet of paper.

'I'll drop you at the police station when I go past,' he said curtly, scanning the page. 'I haven't time to come with you. I'm in court at ten and the case will probably last most of the day.'

With anguished eyes, Lisa stared back at him.

'But what am I going to do, Fergus?' she cried. 'He's watching the house. He has to be. How else would he know about the policemen? He was out there last night all the time they were searching. And they didn't even see him.'

50

CHAPTER SIX

As always, Lisa had to drop Zoe at school on her way to the office and this morning, she would have to speak to someone.

'We'll have to leave a bit earlier, Fergus. I need to speak to Mrs Tompkins. Warn her. She mustn't let Zoe go with anyone, unless it's Moira or me.'

Afterwards, Fergus dropped her at the police station, and she watched his car draw away from the kerb and vanish into the dense commuter traffic. Behind her, swing doors opened, then closed again.

'Hello. What are you doing here?' Alex Miller's smoke-grey eyes smiled into hers as she spun round at the welcome sound of his voice.

'Another letter,' she said flatly, and fished in her bag for the envelope.

'Marc?' he questioned, and she saw his eyes were no longer friendly, but narrowed to cold slits.

When she nodded, he caught her elbow and steered her into the reception area.

'I'll come with you.'

Her body instinctively flinched and his hand dropped away as she retorted sharply, 'Shouldn't you be at the office by now? It won't look too good if you're late on only your

51

second day.'

He gave a rueful laugh. 'Somehow, I don't think anyone's likely to complain. I've been down here at the police station since half-past seven. A client of Tom's decided to do a little larceny during the early hours, but unwittingly chose a house where the son was home on leave from the army. So, instead of finding an elderly couple, deep in sleep, he encountered a keen-eared, young stalwart, who put a half nelson on him and rang the police. Guess what excuse the old lad used?'

'A friend of a friend said I could kip here, and be blowed if I haven't lorst the key. Had to get in through a window, guv, and then to me horror, it was the wrong house?' she replied with a faint smile.

'Right first time! You've obviously heard it all before.'

'It's the standard one round here. It wasn't a man called Olly Bean, was it?'

'Yes, it was,' Alex replied. 'Why, do you know him?'

'He's quite a regular. Been in and out of prison ever since he was a lad. It's his way of life. Straight out and back to stealing again. Not that he's ever had much of a chance. His mother spent most of her life in Holloway.'

'So, my brilliant defence isn't going to carry much weight.' Alex laughed.

'With a record like his?'

As soon as Lisa had given her name to the

officer on duty and requested to see the sergeant, she joined Alex on a row of plastic chairs by the wall.

'Olly's not a bad type really,' she said, as she sat down. 'Always does a neat and tidy job; drawers tipped out on to the bed, cupboards emptied on to the floor. If he can't find an open window, then it's a pane of glass neatly cut out and removed with care.'

'He obviously has your sympathy.'

'He's not a villain. There are some who vandalise and turn a place upside down just for sheer badness, and woe betide anyone who tries to stop them. I bet Olly didn't offer any resistance when the soldier son caught him.'

'No, he didn't. Quite upset, he was, when I spoke to him. "Roughed me up, he did, guv, and I wasn't doing no harm," he kept repeating.'

Lisa could tell that Alex was keeping her talking in an effort to divert her mind from the letter, and she was grateful. It was having the desired effect, too. Alex seemed to create an aura of calmness around her. She felt safe and soothed by his presence. And he kept a distance between them, preventing even the slightest contact. That comforted her as well. He understood.

*   *   *

They had to wait half an hour for the sergeant,

and then he studied the letter without making any comment.

'What are you going to do?' Lisa demanded, annoyed by his silence.

'Letters don't mean a great deal, Miss Callington.'

'But this is a written threat,' she retorted.

'Merely meant to scare you.'

'And succeeding,' Alex added quietly.

Turning his head slowly, the sergeant looked at him.

'Are you a member of Miss Callington's family, sir?'

Alex's jaw tightened. 'No, sergeant, I'm not.'

'Boyfriend?'

'Miss Callington and I work in the same legal practice.'

The policeman raised his eyebrows and smiled slightly.

'Oh,' he said, and the brief word was laced with sarcasm.

Lisa watched a nerve throb in Alex's taut cheek, but he contained his anger.

'So what are you intending to do?' he enquired.

'The fingerprints on the previous note have been checked.'

'And?' Lisa snapped.

'They are those of Marc Coursier.'

'I told you they would be.' Lisa's face was devoid of any colour now.

Drawing a thin folder towards him, the

sergeant opened it. The first envelope lay inside, paper-clipped to its letter. He added the second to it, then looked up at Lisa's enquiring face.

'Thank you, Miss Callington.' Pushing back his chair, he stood up and moved to the door.

Lisa refused to acknowledge the unspoken dismissal.

'My daughter and I are in danger, sergeant.' Her voice quivered and she made an effort to keep it steady. 'Do you intend to wait until Marc Coursier carries out his threat before you take any action?'

'All he implies is that he wants to see his child, Miss Callington. And he is the father.'

' "I shall have my child" were the actual words of his first letter, sergeant,' Alex pointed out. 'Rather a different interpretation, don't you think? And from a man who has just been released from a prison sentence for manslaughter.'

'Released early on account of good behaviour, and now, understandably, he wishes to see his daughter. Not an unusual request for a father, is it?'

'It is when he was denied access to Zoe,' Lisa burst out hotly.

'He has been inside for five years, Miss Callington. That length of time changes a man.'

'Not Marc! Nothing could change him,' she blazed. 'All that prison sentence will have done is add to his need for revenge. He hated me when he went in! Nothing will have changed that. I demand that you arrange a constant watch on both my daughter and myself.'

'Demand, Miss Callington?' The sergeant's pale blue eyes stared unwaveringly at her.

'Demand!' she bit out, meeting his stare.

He closed the file with a snap of sound and replaced it on top of a pile at the back of his desk.

'If I had the manpower, Miss Callington, that heap wouldn't be there. If I had the manpower, the crime rate in this town would easily be halved. If I had the manpower, you'd be dealing with far more clients that you are at present. This man is out to scare you, Miss Callington, nothing more. He's just been released from prison and one thing I can assure you of is—he doesn't intend to return there.' His tone became mild.

'There's no need for you to worry, Miss Callington. No need at all. All he wants to do is put the frighteners on you. Make you stew a little. And you're reacting in exactly the way he wants.'

Lisa regarded him doubtfully. Maybe he's right, she thought. After five years, Marc wouldn't want to go back to prison. Five years is a long time. Especially for a man like Marc. She picked up her bag and turned to Alex.

'We'd better go.'

'If any harm comes to Miss Callington or

her daughter—'

The sergeant interrupted before Alex could say more. 'It won't,' he said curtly and held open the door.

'From now on,' she told Alex after they came out of the police station and returned to the office, 'I'm taking and collecting Zoe from school. It's not that I don't think Moira capable, but if Marc is hanging around, then I'm the one to recognise him. Moira has no idea what he looks like. She's never met him.'

'After five years, will you recognise him?'

It was something that hadn't occurred to her. She remembered Marc as he had been when she first saw him. She had an image of a tall, somewhat grand figure, narrow-hipped, in tight, blue jeans, his powerful shoulders and arms hidden beneath a loose-fitting sweatshirt.

He had stood out among the other students. There was a charisma about him, a strange enchantment that drew her. Exactly what, she couldn't pin down.

His eyes had always attracted her, with their haunting, hypnotic depths. She had loved the way he spoke, his French accent making the most simple words in English seem magical. There was no doubt that she had been fascinated by him, or perhaps infatuated might be a better way of describing how she felt.

Then he had been twenty. Two years of marriage had scarcely changed him, but now, at twenty-seven, would he be different?

'Well? Will you recognise him?' Alex repeated.

Her brow wrinkled. 'I don't know. Maybe I've changed, too.'

But the thought lingered in her mind that she could pass Marc in the street and not know. But no, of course I'd recognise him, she told herself impatiently. How could I ever forget? And her skin prickled into goose-pimples.

*   *   *

After she'd given Zoe her tea that evening, and left her playing Snakes and Ladders with Moira in the lounge, Lisa went upstairs and lifted down an old shoebox from the top shelf of her wardrobe. It was a place her daughter couldn't reach. Dust covered the white cardboard and she blew it off, then undid the tape tied round it. For a long while she sat on the covers of her bed, staring down at the lid, then swiftly removed it.

Why do I keep all this, she reflected. Why?

But once upon a time its contents had been precious. Full of memories. Memories that she thought she would always treasure. Her fingers hesitated as she reached into the box.

She lifted out a rose, in bud, its folded scarlet petals dry and crisp, their colour faded, but still with a lingering, delicate fragrance that trailed the air.

Her wedding day, hers and Marc's . . .

No shimmering gown. No white, drifting veil. Just a summer dress—not even new. But she'd been so happy—then.

Two photographs lay beneath the rose, and as she touched it, the petals suddenly scattered into fragments. Like confetti, she thought.

As she picked up the first photograph, Marc smiled back, standing beside the girl she once was. Our wedding day. A registrar's office in their university town. No family. Just a few friends. And one of them had taken the photograph.

'Must have a record of you tying the knot,' she remembered him saying, but who he was, she couldn't recall.

Was it really love I felt then, she wondered, studying the picture for some clue, or was it that Marc was the most devastating man I'd ever met, and I was terrified of losing him?

The second photograph was of Zoe. Was she really so tiny? So perfect. Peacefully asleep, lashes resting on softly-curved cheeks, fine down covering her little head. Marc had taken that one, she remembered, the day she was born.

He was so proud of her. His child. My daughter. She could hear his voice even now. My daughter, not ours, she recalled.

And, a year later, how he fought for custody of her. It wasn't me he wanted then, only Zoe. If the divorce court hadn't refused his plea . . .

Lisa shuddered, and the photograph slipped from her fingers.

With blurred eyes, she tipped the rest of the contents of the box on to the bed-covers, strewing them across.

A crumpled ticket for a pop concert—that was where she'd first spoken to Marc. The programme of a play. They'd sat in the gallery, hardly able to hear a word, but then words didn't matter—only that she was with Marc.

How could I have been such a fool, she asked herself bitterly. Why didn't I realise? Those sudden changes of mood. One minute passionate, the next remote . . . even then, Marc was taking drugs . . . but I had no idea.

Everything in the box held memories which she'd treasured. With a determined sweep of her hand, she pushed all the bits and pieces into an empty plastic bag, leaving only the picture of Zoe on the bed.

And then, reluctantly, she retrieved Marc's photograph. Zoe has a right to that, she thought—one day.

CHAPTER SEVEN

'When's Alex coming?' Zoe demanded, when Lisa went back into the lounge and the game of Snakes and Ladders was over.

'Mr Miles, dear,' Moira chided. 'Not Alex.'

60

'When's he coming, Mummy? I told him it was Bruno's birthday and he said he would.'

'Mr Miles is far too busy to remember a teddy-bear's birthday, Zoe,' Moira observed, as she picked up the counters and folded the board into its box.

'He will,' Zoe replied, taking the game from her and putting it in the bureau drawer. 'He said so. I'll go and wait by the gate.'

'No!' Lisa's voice was sharp. 'You're staying indoors.'

'But I don't want to stay indoors,' the little girl protested. 'You haven't let me play in the garden at all today.'

Lisa exchanged glances with Moira. With Marc's threat hanging over them, no way could they let Zoe out of their sight for one second.

'It's bedtime soon,' Lisa reminded her.

'After I've had a go on the swing, please, Mummy.'

'Five minutes, that's all, and I'll come out and push you.'

It was still warm in the garden, with the scent of late narcissi drifting sweetly in the evening air, to mingle with the heady fragrance of lilac.

'Bruno can have a swing, too, 'cos it's his birthday,' Zoe announced, tucking the bear beside her as she climbed on to the swaying seat.

'Not too high,' Lisa warned, 'or Bruno will fall off.'

61

There was a wooden bench under the hedge of rhododendrons and she settled herself on it, closing her eyes as she enjoyed the sunshine. Early May had been hot like this for the past two or three years, she recalled. Perhaps we're in for another baking summer.

A car engine sounded in the lane outside and Lisa tensed.

'Alex has come!' Zoe sang out. 'I can see him over the top of the lilac trees.'

Lisa jerked to her feet.

The little girl slowed the swing and jumped off, running across the lawn towards the front of the house.

'Wait!' Lisa shouted urgently.

'But it's Alex, Mummy.'

By the time Lisa had caught up with them, Alex was lifting the child high in the air, swinging her round.

'I told Mummy you'd come but she didn't believe me.'

Lisa found herself lost in the warmth of his eyes as he smiled at her.

'I couldn't stay away,' he said softly.

'Come and have a cup of tea,' Zoe instructed, taking his hand.

'May I?' he asked, his gaze on Lisa.

'Well,' she replied, grudgingly, 'I suppose, now that you're here . . . '

'I'd like to see Fergus, too. Is he back yet? There are a few points I need to sort out with him before he gets embroiled in that fraud case over at Lewes. He'll be in court there for the rest of the week.'

'He should be home any time now,' Lisa said, glancing at the clock as they went through the hall.

'And I've brought a present for Bruno. Is he allowed to eat jelly babies?' Alex enquired, squatting down on his haunches beside Zoe.

'He's still on the swing,' the little girl replied, darting away from them. 'I'll go and fetch him, then you can see.'

As Zoe went out of the back door, Fergus entered by the front, and the sudden draught made every door in the house slam shut.

'Sorry about that,' Fergus apologised, carefully placing his briefcase on a chair, and sinking into another. 'What a day!'

'As bad as that?' Alex laughed.

'Worse! All we got was an adjournment for two weeks. What a waste of a day! And then, of course, I'm off to Lewes tomorrow. Goodness knows when I'm going to get into the office. Thank goodness you're there to cope, Alex.'

Moira poured him a large glass of sherry, and offered one to Alex, who shook his head.

'So, what did the police say about that letter you received this morning, my dear?' Fergus asked, taking the glass and sipping it slowly.

'They're checking for fingerprints,' Lisa replied.

'And?'

'That's it!'

'Nothing more?'

She shook her head. 'I wanted a watch put on the house, but the sergeant refused.'

I doubt he'd consider it necessary. After all, there's always someone here with you,' Fergus said, draining his glass, and replacing it on the small table beside his chair.

'But what about Zoe at school?' Lisa demanded, her voice rising in agitation.

'You've warned Mrs Tompkins. She's a very sensible sort of woman from what you say, isn't she?'

'I hope so,' Lisa said. 'The sergeant's positive that Marc is only trying to frighten us—and won't attempt anything at all.'

'Probably quite right, too,' Fergus observed, getting up to pour more sherry. 'It is five years, my dear. And the man has only just been released from prison. He'll not want to return there in a hurry.'

Lisa's fingers knotted. 'That's what the sergeant keeps saying, but none of you know what Marc's like. He adored Zoe. And he thought with all the money his family possesses, he'd easily gain custody of her.' She turned to look appealingly at Fergus. 'You saw, and heard him in the divorce court when custody was refused. If that man lays his hands on Zoe, I shall never see her again.' Her expression suddenly changed to one of alarm. 'Where is Zoe? Is she still in the garden?'

Alex was first out of the door, running down the path, calling the child's name. Lisa followed, clusters of lilac whipping across her face as she raced after him, every beat of her heart resounding in her ears like a note of doom.

At the far end of the garden the swing swayed. And on the grass beside it lay the teddy-bear. The silence was complete.

'Zoe!' The sound that tore from Lisa's throat was a cry of raw anguish.

Alex's arm closed round her shoulders, drawing her into his side, his cheek against hers. And, for once, she remained there, unmoving, her body limp, sagging like a rag doll.

'What's happened?' Panting wildly, Fergus arrived, red-faced and perspiring.

Lisa shook her head silently, tears cascading down her cheeks, her teeth biting into her lower lip, drawing blood.

'She may just be playing a game, hiding from us.' Moira joined them by the swing. 'You know what Zoe's like, always full of mischief.'

'I think you'd better call the police, Fergus,' Alex suggested. 'Straight away.'

He eased Lisa away from his side, studying her face as he said gently, 'Go back indoors with Moira. I'm going to search the lanes. There may be a car.'

'You won't find him.' Lisa's voice was wooden, toneless.

'If he's anywhere out there, I will,' Alex retorted grimly.

He squeezed her cold hand, then was gone, leaving a trail of shivering leaves behind him along the path.

Lisa stood, watching him go.

'He won't ever find her. No-one will. Marc will make quite sure of that.'

CHAPTER EIGHT

The lanes echoed with the strident wail of sirens as police patrol cars came and went. The noise filled the air with its eerie sound.

'Why don't they stop?' Lisa implored, clasping her hands to her ears.

'The police have to keep searching, and they're sure to find her, dear,' Moira encouraged, picking up the tray. 'Shall I make some more tea?'

'If I see another cup of tea, I'll scream,' Lisa said harshly.

'Moira's only trying to help, Lisa.'

'I know, Fergus. I'm sorry.' Lisa's nails dug into the fabric of the chair. 'But none of this is going to bring back Zoe.'

'Of course it will,' Fergus retorted, leaning across to pat the back of her hand. 'Cheer up now. You're being defeatist.'

The front doorbell rang and she ran into the

hall, her fingers struggling with the catch.

'Let me,' Fergus said, opening the door.

Shoulders slumped, Alex stood there.

'I'm sorry,' he said, looking straight at Lisa, his eyes full of compassion.

Headlights blazed through the trees, casting shadows, as cars swept up the drive, and the sergeant appeared, looking weary.

'No luck, I'm afraid, Miss Callington. Do you mind if I come inside? Perhaps, if we put our heads together, we can come up with something.'

'If you'd taken action right at the beginning, none of this would have happened,' Lisa rapped out bitterly.

'In retrospect, I can only agree, Miss Callington, but it's no use looking backwards, is it? Now we have to forge ahead. I'd like some details about your ex-husband.'

'Isn't it all in your file?' she enquired, her voice tinged with sarcasm.

'Lisa,' Alex murmured from behind her, his lips brushing the lobe of her ear as he spoke, 'you're not making things easy.'

'I'm sorry. It's just . . . ' Her mouth trembled and she fought to control it.

'We know,' the sergeant said, and she was surprised at the unexpected gentleness of his tone. 'But to find your daughter now, we do need all the help we can get.'

Her voice steadied. 'What do you want me to tell you?'

'Coursier was a violent man. To you, or everyone?'

'What you really want to know is—did Marc ever harm Zoe, isn't it, sergeant? No,' she said, shaking her head. 'Never. He loved her. Truly adored her. He seemed quite awed by her fragility.'

'And the child was only a baby when you left him? How old?'

'Almost six months.'

'Would you say your daughter was a quiet child?'

Lisa gave a rueful little laugh and glanced at Moira. 'Zoe can be quite a handful at times, can't she?' Her eyes widened with growing horror. 'You don't think Marc would . . .'

'I'm sure he won't,' the sergeant replied hastily. 'You said he was very fond of the child.'

'But she was a baby then. Now she can be quite determined at times.'

'Takes after you, perhaps?'

'Like me?' Lisa questioned, staring at him. And Marc hated me, she remembered.

'Shouldn't we be trying to work out where Marc will take Zoe?' Alex put in quickly.

'Well, he's only just been released from prison,' the sergeant said. 'I've asked for any information about what arrangements were made for him by his family. They may have hired a car for him, and perhaps a flat. His father is in the property market, isn't he, Miss

68

Callington? You and your ex-husband were involved in the business,' he prompted.

She nodded. 'When we first went to France, Marc and I travelled round locating derelict buildings for Pierre to buy and renovate. He paid our travelling expenses and a small commission—not a great deal, but enough for us to live on over there.'

'And you said his father also bought properties in Britain, didn't you?'

'Yes. In the West Country—Devon and Cornwall. There were plenty of cottages and old barns around then. It's tailed off since the recession I should imagine, with fewer people buying, especially second homes.'

Alex sank his chin into his hands. 'So, if Marc wanted somewhere to hide out, it's doubtful he'd go to France, knowing there could be a check at the ports for him. He might choose a place his father owns in Britain.'

'He might,' the sergeant agreed, looking hopeful.

'Could you obtain a list of the properties Pierre Coursier has for sale?'

'It's an idea.'

'If Miss Callington or I can be of any help . . .' Alex added. 'We're both well versed in conveyancing, so we could save you a bit of time checking through the details.'

'I'll find out which bank Coursier deals with,' the sergeant mused, rubbing his nose.

'Pop into the station in the morning. I'll have the bank fax the property list direct to me there.'

* * *

To Lisa, it was the longest night she'd ever experienced. She couldn't sleep. Every detail of Zoe's short life filled her mind. The day she was born in that little French hospital, with nuns flitting to and fro. She'd wondered whether they envied each mother, possessing a child—something they could never have. Or did they regard every baby born as if their own? They had a wealth of love and kindness.

Zoe was such an active baby, right from the start; never lying peacefully in her cot or pram like other children, always alert. Everyone said she would be a bright child, and they were right. She's way ahead of her age group at school, Mrs Tompkins says. Full of curiosity. Always asking questions. Eager to learn. Never still.

Lisa remembered the long trek across France to Cherbourg, dreading that at any minute Marc would appear, full of pent-up fury. It was only as the ferry glided out into the open sea that relief finally flooded over her.

From Portsmouth, she'd caught a train to London, then on to her own home town, only to be told that her parents were already on their way to France.

I should never have mentioned what Marc was doing to me, she regretted. But when they'd spoken on the telephone one night, everything had poured out in a torrent of despair.

At the same time as she was packing to escape, they had decided to come to France and fetch her home. And then, soon after arriving at Cherbourg, their car had been in a collision . . .

It was all my fault. My fault. If only I'd never told them. If only I'd left Marc sooner. They would still be alive today. And it's my fault Zoe's missing. All my fault.

The thoughts went round and round in her mind, twisting and turning, always arriving back at the same point.

My fault. My fault . . .

*   *   *

'Isn't Mr McDonald here to accompany you, Miss Callington?' the sergeant enquired, giving Alex a hard look when they arrived the following morning.

'Fergus is in court at Lewes for the rest of the week,' she replied wearily. 'It's an important case—fraud—he has to be there.'

More important than my daughter, she silently added. He'd been quite adamant that he must be in court. It had saddened Lisa.

'Well, here's the list of Pierre Coursier's

71

properties in England. The bank held a copy. A lot of their money is invested in Pierre Coursier, one way or another.'

Alex leaned his long body against the desk as he scanned the pages.

'Quite a number of properties. Well scattered, too. That doesn't help.'

'Are any in the process of rebuilding?' Lisa asked, resting on her elbows as she studied the list.

'You mean Marc wouldn't use a property that was seething with workmen?' Alex said.

She nodded.

The sergeant frowned.

'How do we tell that?'

'Here, in this column. It shows money paid over to contractors. Look, this one on Bodmin Moor must be well on the way to completion. Four thousand pounds to a roofing firm.' Her interest grew as her gaze travelled the page. 'And this one, near Penzance, has a sum for rewiring. Both were paid over only a week ago, so work must still be going on.'

She turned to the next sheet.

'There's another here, at Falmouth. Money paid to a plastering firm. These properties all have work in progress, so Marc probably wouldn't stay in any of them.'

'Well, that whittles the number down quite a bit.' Alex nodded. 'Only five possibles left.'

'But which one will Marc use?' she agonised.

'If he goes to any of them at all,' the sergeant muttered. 'Let's have some tea. I can see this will be a long morning.'

While the sergeant was out of the room, Alex rapidly jotted down the addresses, and slipped the notebook back into the pocket of his jacket. The sergeant returned, carrying a biscuit-tin lid on which rested three, thin plastic beakers.

'Five properties. Well-spaced out, too.' The sergeant stirred the beakers with a spoon then handed them round. 'Oh, there is one thing—I can confirm that Coursier has transport. We've questioned his father. He picked him up after his release and took him to Guildford where he'd converted a property into furnished flats which he lets out. He set aside one for his son when he heard he was up for release. And he provided him with a car.'

Alex groaned.

'So he could be anywhere by now,' Lisa said hollowly.

'He can't travel too far with a young child in tow,' the sergeant reassured her. 'Not if she's like any of the kids I've come into contact with. My own two were bad enough, but the grandchildren . . . well . . .'

How can he talk about her in such a detached manner, Lisa wondered. She's my daughter, Zoe. But to the police I suppose she's merely a case, like the cases we work on in the office, completely impersonal. It's how one has to work to avoid becoming emotionally involved. Life would be unbearable if you did.

'Right then, Miss Callington, I'll have someone check out these addresses. If your daughter's at any of them, we'll soon have her home safely.'

And what will Marc's reaction be to that, she wondered. Police hammering on the door. Everything she'd ever heard about hostages and sieges spiralled through her mind.

She felt Alex's fingers lightly grip her elbow, drawing her towards the door and a protest rose to her lips. But, as if sensing it, he said quickly, 'Thank you, sergeant. We'd better get back home and leave everything in your hands. I know you'll contact us when you have definite news.'

The door closed behind them, and she twisted out of his grasp.

'I'm not leaving anything in his hands,' she blazed.

'Neither am I,' Alex replied calmly.

'But you said . . . '

'What I said and what I intend to do are two entirely different things.' He tugged open the car door. 'We could easily be on the wrong track, you know, Lisa. Are you prepared to take that risk?'

She hesitated on the edge of the kerb. 'What are you intending to do?'

'How will Marc react when he sees police

outside his door?'

'That's what's been worrying me,' she replied.

'And what conclusion did you reach?'

'Either he'll turn violent, or lie low.'

'So, neither way are the police going to find Zoe.'

'No,' she agreed.

'Then it's up to us, isn't it?'

'Us?' she queried.

'You and me, Lisa.'

'But what about your work? You're supposed to be standing in for Tom. Isn't that important to you? You can't just toss everything aside for some strange child, Alex.'

'Zoe's not some strange child to me, Lisa. She's your child. And as for work, now, make up your mind quickly. I'm wasting precious time. Are you coming with me, or not?'

'I'm coming.'

'Hop in then.'

The car door slammed shut and as Alex slid his long frame into the seat beside her, she heard the engine roar into life.

'There's a road atlas tucked under the dashboard in front of you, and here's the list,' he said, tossing the notebook into her lap. 'Work out which of those properties is nearest, then you can do some navigating. At the moment I'm heading west. The rest is up to you.'

CHAPTER NINE

Lisa ran a finger down the map index. She flipped quickly through the pages of the road atlas until she found the right one.

'Bideford, not far from Barnstaple, on the north Devon coast. You'll need to aim for Exeter, then go up from there.' A note of despair crept into her voice. 'It's going to take us hours, Alex.'

'And it's going to take Marc hours as well, don't forget.'

'If he is travelling this way.'

'Look, we've got to start somewhere, haven't we, Lisa? It's a gamble, whatever we do. If you'd rather go back and wait for police results, then I'll take you, but after I've done so, I'll head back to the West Country.'

'And I'm coming with you,' she said fiercely.

He kept his gaze on the road ahead, but she saw his mouth widen into a smile. We will find her, Lisa. I promise you that.'

Slowly, oh so slowly, she watched the miles roll by. The outskirts of Chichester came and went, the cathedral spire towering in the distance, followed by the marshy wastes bordering Southsea and Portsmouth.

'Are you in love with Fergus?' Alex's question came out of the blue, jarring into her.

'He's a part of my family,' she said. 'I've

known him for a long time.'

'But do you love him?'

The car changed lanes and overtook a crowded coach. Lisa saw a child wave from one of its windows, and for a moment her heart stilled, until she realised it was a fair-haired, little boy.

'Fergus has been extremely kind to me all my life—and so was Sheila.'

'Like a father and mother to you?' Alex prompted softly.

'Yes,' she agreed. 'You could say that.'

'So, why marry him? Why not let him remain a father figure?'

Her lip began to tremble. 'I can't live in his house, now that Sheila is dead. It would put him in a difficult position, with the job he has.'

'You could move out.' He paused, then went on. 'Or is it that you need the security?'

'Security?'

'Fergus is like a father to you—that's what you implied. Someone who will look after you. Keep you safe. And you haven't a father of your own now.'

She wound the window down a little and let the wind blow across her face.

'I owe a lot to Fergus,' she said defensively.

'Marriage is a high price to pay, Lisa.'

'We shall continue to live exactly as we are. Nothing will change.'

She saw his mouth turn down at the corners. 'Oh.'

'What do you mean by that?' she demanded, pushing a strand of hair away from her cheek with an impatient gesture.

'So how do you live now?'

'We don't live together, if that's what you're hinting at. All we do is live under the same roof.'

'I didn't suggest you were lovers.'

'But you implied it,' she retorted hotly. 'What you forget is, I can't even bear a man to touch me, let alone make love to me.'

'Not every man is like Marc, Lisa.'

'I know,' she replied. 'Fergus isn't.'

'And with Fergus you'll always be safe, is that it?' Alex twisted the steering-wheel as a lorry veered across their path. 'Do you honestly think Fergus won't want to make love to you?'

'He still loves Sheila,' she said fiercely.

'Do you regret that?'

'Of course I don't!' she raged. 'It's what I want.'

'Never to be loved? Never to love?' he said gently, his gaze still on the busy road ahead. 'Is that what you really want, Lisa?'

Through tear-misted eyes, she stared out through the window into the pale green freshness of New Forest trees as they passed.

'Yes, Alex,' she answered. 'That's exactly what I want.'

*   *   *

It was late afternoon when they reached Bideford, crossing the new bridge over the river and winding down into the town. Alex had insisted they stop to eat halfway through their journey, despite all Lisa's protests. But she was glad they did, biting into thick ham rolls with a hunger she hadn't imagined. Afterwards, she felt calmer.

'So what address are we looking for?'

'It's a farmhouse,' she said, checking the notebook. 'We'd better ask someone. It could be on either side of the town.'

The first three people had never heard of it, or were only visiting Devon, but Alex eventually found a post office and enquired there.

'It's back the way we've come,' he said, climbing into the car and edging it away from the kerb. 'A mile or so from Instow.'

The lane was off the main road, very narrow, with high, grassy banks and hedges, part-hiding the farm. A golden retriever rushed towards them, barking, when the car bumped over the cobbles of the yard.

'Someone's here,' Alex commented.

'The whole place does appear to be lived in,' Lisa agreed, looking at the fresh, whitewashed buildings forming three sides of a square around them.

'Can I help you?' A woman, middle-aged, and cheerful, came out, wiping her hands on a towel.

'We thought this place was up for sale.' Alex lowered the car window to speak to her.

The woman smiled. 'It was. We only moved in a week ago. My husband and I have retired down here. The adjoining granary's been turned into an annexe to let as holiday flats and we shall do bed and breakfast in the main part of the house. I only hope it all works out.'

'You've no-one staying here yet then?' Alex enquired.

'Not for a week or so. Most of the new furniture has yet to arrive—and the bedding. Why, were you interested? You're the second people to drive in today.'

'The second?'

'Yes. A man and his little girl came by an hour or so ago.'

'Little girl?' Lisa opened the door of the car and jumped out. 'What did she look like?'

The woman gave her a curious glance. 'The fellow took off as soon as I came out, but I could see a child curled up asleep on the back seat. Pretty hair. Your sort of colour.'

'Zoe!' Lisa cried, turning to Alex. 'It has to be.'

'Someone you know?' the woman asked, restraining the dog as it began to lick Lisa's wrist.

'My daughter! She's been kidnapped.'

Alarm filled the woman's eyes. 'Kidnapped?'

'We can't be sure it's Zoe,' Alex warned, his fingers closing over Lisa's clenched hand. 'Can you describe the man?'

'I only caught a glimpse as he turned the car. Dark hair, late twenties, early thirties, maybe. Quite striking looks.'

'Marc!' Lisa breathed.

Alex tugged her back into the car and started to reverse. 'Thanks for your help,' he called, as they shot backwards out of the yard into the lane.

'It must have been Zoe, mustn't it?'

'Don't raise your hopes too much, Lisa,' he pleaded. 'We'll contact the local police and they can get in touch with the sergeant back home. And he can tell Fergus and Moira where we are.'

*   *   *

'The sergeant wasn't over the moon when he heard we were down here, was he?' Alex remarked wryly as they left the police station behind them and continued westwards.

'We've made more progress than he has. At least he has something to work on now, although I can't understand why no-one's traced the car. Marc's father must have given them its registration number.'

'Maybe he's changed it. Or hired one,' Alex suggested.

Lisa opened the map again. 'Hartland

Point's only about twenty or so miles. The next property's in that area. It looks pretty remote, so they could be there, couldn't they, Alex?'

'Lisa, it might not have been Marc and Zoe the woman saw. Please don't raise your hopes too high.'

'I can't help it,' she answered bleakly. 'Without hope . . . '

His fingers enfolded hers, smoothing the skin.

'I know,' he said gently. 'I know.'

*   *   *

Light was already fading as the car approached the headland overlooking the sea and began to descend the steep hill to the quay. Around them the air vibrated with the thunder of wave against rock.

Lisa remembered coming here as a child, protesting loudly after a visit to Clovelly that they'd seen no donkeys climbing its cobbled street.

It seemed so long ago. I couldn't have been any older than Zoe, she reflected. Zoe. She closed her eyes, visualising the image of her little daughter. The poor mite would be terrified, alone with a stranger. How would Marc treat her? Would the love he'd once had still remain?

And if it doesn't . . . agony speared through Lisa.

'We will find her,' Alex said softly, once again sensing her fears, as he stopped the car beside the sea wall to ask directions from a little shop. A rosy little woman stepped outside, to point the way.

'You'll have to walk from here. Along that path there. 'Tis only a cottage. Thinking of buying, were you? 'Tis in a poor state. Not been lived in since old Tremaine died, oh, two or mebbe three year ago.'

The path was overgrown, brambles trailing thickly on either side, catching at their clothes and skin. Clusters of pink thrift clung to granite, lichen-covered rocks that rose through the short, wind-swept grass, and here and there a lone harebell swayed.

When they eventually found the cottage, they could tell no-one was there. The walls were part-tumbled, slates fallen from the roof, and through the salt-hazed broken glass of the windows the rooms inside were desolate.

With the sea breeze whipping her hair into a confusion around her, Lisa stood forlornly, suddenly overwhelmed with despair. Marc had succeeded. They were never going to find Zoe. Tears blinded her eyes and she turned to Alex, weeping out her torment, and was held in the comfort of his shoulder as his arms closed round her.

The tweed of his jacket prickled her cheek, the rhythmic sweep of his fingers smoothing the nape of her neck. His mouth brushed across her eyelids, and she kept them closed, not daring to meet his gaze, frightened what her own would reveal.

His hand stroked across her forehead, lifting away tangled strands of hair, and that fleeting touch sent a wave of fire coursing through her.

Reluctantly, she pushed away from him, fighting a desire to stay there, caught in the safety of his arms.

'We should go on,' she said. 'Marc must be somewhere.'

'Tomorrow,' Alex breathed, the words feathering warmth across her skin.

'No,' she pleaded. 'We must catch up with them.'

'You're exhausted, Lisa. Rest now. Just for a while.'

'How can I ever rest, until I find Zoe?' she anguished.

He bent his head, his lips touching her hair.

'Tomorrow, Lisa. Tomorrow. It's late now. Marc will have to stop, too.'

Persuaded, she let him lead her back along the cliffs to the car. They sat there, with the windows lowered, watching night creep over the sea. A pinpoint of light twinkled far in the inky distance, like a star fallen from the myriad above.

She could hear waves encircling the rocks below, and her tongue tasted their salt on her lips. Beside her, Alex was silent, his outline a silhouette. From the hunch of his shoulders, she realised that he, too, was tired, and felt guilty for making him travel so far.

It would be daylight again around five. Maybe, if they both slept until then . . .

*   *   *

A stiffness in her neck woke her. For a moment, she couldn't work out where she was. Awkwardly, she moved her head, and discovered it was resting in the crook of Alex's arm.

His breathing was rhythmic, lips slightly parted. Stubble darkened his chin and around his mouth. A lock of fair hair fell over his forehead and she thought how vulnerable and defenceless he looked in sleep. He was like a small child.

A small child . . . the agony of losing Zoe swamped over her again.

A thin line of silver edged the horizon, defining sea from sky. The clock on the dashboard of the car showed ten minutes to five.

Where was Zoe now? What terror was she feeling? Lisa pressed her lips together, biting back the misery that lay behind them. What use were tears?

Alex stirred, his arm drawing her closer. She felt the slight pressure of his jaw against her hair. There was no way she could move away

85

without wakening him and yet, she didn't want to move away. The steady beat of his heart throbbed against her ear and the warmth of him radiated through her, arousing her body in a way she'd forgotten.

In a month I shall be married to Fergus, she reminded herself, and his ring was suddenly tight around her finger like a bond.

CHAPTER TEN

'It's going to take three to four hours at least to reach Helston,' Alex told her, once they were back on the road again. 'You're quite sure there aren't any more properties listed in between?'

'Look for yourself if you don't believe me.'

The cleft in his chin deepened as he smiled.

'I believe you,' he said. 'And we're stopping to eat once we find somewhere that's open.' He ran his fingers over his chin as he spoke, frowning at the rasp of sound. 'Preferably somewhere that sells throw-away razors.'

'A wash wouldn't go amiss either,' she murmured. 'For both of us.'

By the time they reached Bodmin Moor, the sun was highlighting the yellow gorse, and sending cloud shadows chasing over the hills.

At a service station earlier, they'd had breakfast and now felt refreshed again. As the car zoomed on towards Truro, Lisa's spirits started to rise.

Today they were going to find Zoe. She was positive of that. She refused to let her mind even think of the alternative.

'How far now?'

'To Helston?' Alex asked. 'That last signpost said nine miles. Fifteen minutes or so, I should say.'

Around them the countryside stretched green into the distance on either side. Every so often, small villages clustered beside the road. Derelict engine-houses rose here and there indicating where, centuries before, copper and tin mines had flourished.

At the outskirts of the town, the sound of a band stirred in the air, a drum thudding out the beat.

'What's the date?' Alex said suddenly, slowing the car into a queue of traffic.

'Date? Oh, May seventh, I think. No, it's May eighth. Why?'

'Flora Day!'

Lisa stared blankly at him.

'Helston. The Furry Dance, eighth May. The whole town grinds to a halt. There's no way we're going to get through. Let's find somewhere to park the car, and we'll walk. Where's the property we're looking for?'

'Meneage Street. A shop with a flat above.'

'Right in the centre of town. I went camping on the Lizard once, years back, with a gang from university. We travelled into Helston for food. I remember there's a big supermarket just off Wendron Street. We'll park the car there.'

'But Zoe . . . '

'Lisa, if they're in the town, they can't avoid the dancing. That flat overlooks one of the main streets.'

* * *

Everywhere there were crowds, lining the pavements or meandering through the narrow, flag-bedecked roads. Swathes of greenery and bluebells decorated the houses and shop-fronts. Windows were filled with spring flowers.

And over the whole town hung the sound of the band.

'Just missed the children's dance,' a laughing woman told them as they threaded their way down from the carpark. 'Main dance is at noon. That's the one to see. You should find a place along here if you can. It all gets a bit overcrowded.'

'What's this street called?' Alex asked her.

'Meneage Street.'

There was a sudden flurry as a group of little girls ran past, their pretty, white dresses swirling.

'Did you enjoy it, Sally-Anne?' the laughing woman called to one child, and was rewarded

88

by an enthusiastic nod.

'The schools are represented by different garlands of flowers for the girls' hair, and all the boys wear a spray of lily of the valley on their white shirts,' the woman explained.

Lisa was only half-listening, her eyes searching the open windows above the shops for her daughter's small face.

'This way.' Alex caught her hand. 'It's that empty shop, down there.'

But before she could move, the sound of the band grew and the crowd suddenly surged forward, taking her with them, parting her from Alex.

The music was deafening now, vibrating round her, each brass instrument a dazzle of brilliance in the sunshine. Behind came a strange shuffling, then the first couple of dancers appeared. Lisa could only stare in admiration. The man wore a grey top hat and dark morning suit; the lady, a long flowing gown of scarlet taffeta, cut low, and a beautiful wide-brimmed hat of stiff, black lace.

Elegantly, they passed, slowly revolving as the dance progressed, followed by the next couple, and the next, and the next. Every gown and hat was different, each one, a splendid creation of colour and style.

The line seemed never-ending and when she thought it must finish, yet another band appeared, followed by more dancing couples.

People pressed forward from all sides,

craning their necks to see, imprisoning her. But, finally, the dancers were gone, only the faint shuffle of their feet and rhythmic echo of the band hanging in the air.

Twisting her neck, Lisa saw Alex, his eyes, now the colour of clouds on a summer's day, smiling down at her. The strange magic of the dance still clung to her, every fibre of her body taut with a whole gamut of emotions, and she smiled back, letting her head rest for a moment against his cheek. And it was as if only the two of them were there. No-one else.

She forgot even Zoe.

Her gaze went to the high window above the shop, but it was closed and blank.

A flicker of movement caught her eye, far back in the room, then it vanished so quickly that she wondered whether she had imagined it.

'There's someone there,' Alex breathed, tugging her towards an alley, so narrow they had to edge sideways to enter it. Builders' debris—bits of wood, broken bricks, a pile of paint tins—lay around the threshold of the door. Alex gave it a push to reveal an empty storeroom, and a flight of stairs leading upwards.

Lisa followed him, climbing two at a time, her breath tight in her throat.

A man in paint-spattered, white overalls regarded them with startled amazement when they burst through the upper door, a long roller dripping in his hand as he jerked round.

'Scared the living daylights out of me,' he grumbled. 'What are you up to, barging in like that?'

Without stopping to apologise, Alex said, 'Are you by any chance working for Pierre Coursier?'

Raising the roller, the painter swept it across a section of the ceiling. 'Might do,' he replied. 'Why?'

'Do you or don't you?' Lisa demanded.

'What's it to you?'

'I am Mrs Coursier!' Lisa snapped, hating to use the name.

'Oh.' The painter looked startled. 'Well, another one of your lot has been in today checking on me. I'm going as fast as I can . . . '

'When?' Alex spat out. 'When was the man here?'

'Must've been before ten o'clock. Kids' dance hadn't started.'

'Did he have a little girl with him?' Lisa asked, her heart thudding.

The painter shrugged. 'Only put his head round the door. Didn't seem as though he expected anyone to be here. Shot off a couple of minutes later when we'd had a word or two.'

'And you didn't see a child?' Alex persisted.

'No.'

Alex leaned his back against the door frame. 'Any idea where he was going?'

'Only other one Coursier's got around here

is out near Coverack. Bought a month or so back. Nothing's been started there yet though. Proper old ruin.'

Lisa and Alex exchanged glances.

'Well, it looks as if you're making a good job of this place,' Alex said, edging Lisa out of the door. 'Mrs Coursier will be able to give a good report to her father-in-law when she sees him.'

'I hope you had your fingers crossed,' Lisa whispered as they raced down the stairs together. 'Telling all those lies.'

'Half-truths.' He grinned. 'Now, back to the car and we're on our way to Coverack.'

'Do you know where it is?'

His grey eyes crinkled. 'Out on the Lizard— three or four miles from where I once stayed.'

CHAPTER ELEVEN

The sound of the car wheels on the road drummed into Lisa's ears. Supposing Zoe isn't there? What am I going to do, she asked herself. How shall I bear it? Hope had kept her going now for two days. Once that hope was gone . . .

She glanced across at Alex as he drove. His profile was like granite, his knuckles white as they gripped the steering-wheel. He's as tense as I am, she thought. And yet, Zoe means nothing to him. Why does he care so much?

It's Fergus who should be here. In a month, I will be his wife. Fergus should be here.

The rush of air through the open car window ruffled Alex's hair. She recalled how he looked when asleep and was filled with a sudden longing to feel his arms round her.

In a month I shall be married to Fergus.

Alex turned his head, reading her eyes, and she saw him shake his head.

'Don't marry Fergus, Lisa,' he said quietly, and she wondered whether she had spoken her thoughts aloud. 'Your life—both your lives— will be impossible if you do.'

'If Zoe's not there . . .' she began, and her voice was lost.

'If Zoe's not there,' he replied, 'we shall continue searching until we do find her, no matter how long it takes.'

'I've never thanked you for bringing me all this way.'

'You don't need to. It's purely selfish—I want to be there to see all your fear dispelled when Zoe's safe again. Fear has always been there, like a barrier between us, hasn't it, Lisa? Once it's gone . . .'

She waited, and the note in his voice was low when he spoke again.

'I always want to be there for you.'

Lisa scarcely noticed the passing scenery, her mind whirling. Alex's words repeated themselves over and over again in her ears.

I always want to be there for you.

The car was snaking down another hill, glimpses of white-flecked waves appearing and disappearing with every twist and turn. Boats lay, swaying on the tide, in the horseshoe curve of the harbour, and a boy leaned over the stone wall, fishing. Windsurfers darted to and fro, like brilliant butterflies skimming the surface of the sea. A small dinghy with an outboard motor trailed empty boards back to the slipway, where a wet-suited figure was waiting to haul them up.

A picture-postcard scene, tranquil and serene, Lisa mused. And then it was suddenly broken by the raucous shrill of sirens. Her skin prickled with apprehension as she scanned the distance ahead.

Two police cars, headlights flashing, were tearing across a field at breakneck speed. With a screech of tyres they shot out through the gate and into the road, then on down towards the harbour.

Someone was running across the cobbled jetty. Lisa's body froze. She recognised the tall, thin figure, there was no mistake.

Alex cut the car's engine.

'Marc?' he questioned, and read the answer in her terrified eyes.

With the police cars almost on top of him, the man veered sideways, down the slipway, pushing aside the wet-suited figure by the dinghy. The outboard motor roared as it swooped in a wide circle away from the jetty

94

and headed out to sea, a trail of spray pluming upwards.

Lisa clutched at the sleeve of Alex's jacket.

'Zoe! Where's Zoe?'

Grimly, Alex restarted the car and headed to where the police vehicles remained, surrounded by a group of curious onlookers.

'Oh, Miss Callington,' came a weary sigh. The police sergeant regarded her dolefully. 'I wish you'd left this to us.'

'Where's Zoe?' she cried, throwing open the car door.

'Just calm down, Miss Callington. Your daughter's quite safe.'

Lisa's eyelids closed, tears seeping, as she buried her head against Alex's chest.

'Where is Zoe?' He repeated the question urgently, soothing her neck with gentle fingers. 'Can't you see the poor girl's frantic about her daughter?'

'I can assure you, she's quite all right, Mr Miles. Would you like me to have the child brought down here? We have a policewoman with her.'

'Of course, we want to see her!' Alex roared.

The sergeant leaned back into the car to speak into a handset.

'Fifteen minutes, and she'll be with you.'

With a reverberating shatter of noise, a helicopter shot from behind the hills and began to circle over the sea. People were

95

already climbing on to the harbour wall, their voices loud, shrill with excitement as they watched.

Clearing a way, the sergeant indicated for Lisa and Alex to follow. They stood by the harbour wall, the stone cool as they rested against its rough surface.

The dinghy was visible only by its wake of spray. Above, the helicopter pursued it like an angry hornet.

'He's heading for the Manacles,' someone shouted.

'In more ways than one,' the sergeant grimaced. 'Vicious rocks,' he explained. 'Caused a lot of shipwrecks over the centuries. Not the best place to choose in a flimsy little craft like that one.'

'Can't someone stop him?' Lisa cried, her eyes wide with horror.

'Bit late now.'

The chatter around them died away, leaving an eerie silence. Everyone waited.

As Lisa watched, the column of spray from the dinghy merged into that of the waves climbing grey-brown rocks far out to sea. The helicopter dropped lower, almost touching the surface, then began to circle round and round. She could hear the drone of its engine rise and fall.

Gradually, the spectators started to drift away. There was a strange, sad atmosphere.

Lisa remained, her eyes stinging with

unshed tears. Once, she remembered, I loved him. Now the sea has him.

Alex's arm was round her shoulders, drawing her away from the wall.

'It's over, Lisa. All over.'

Another police car was bumping over the cobbles, and before it had stopped, Lisa was running, her arms outstretched. She could see Zoe!

Her small, freckled face smudged and bewildered, Zoe stepped out on to the jetty and was caught and held as though Lisa could never let her go again.

'I thought you weren't going to come, Mummy,' the little girl wept, and her tears were lost amongst Lisa's.

'Can we take her home now?' Alex quietly asked the sergeant.

'There's a hotel just along the road, Mr Miles. We'll book rooms there for you all for tonight. I'm afraid we'll have to ask the little girl a few questions, but we'll leave that until she's settled down a bit. Once she's had a good sleep, she'll be as right as ninepence.'

*   *   *

'I always felt, deep in my heart, that Marc wouldn't harm her,' Lisa said later that evening as she and Alex sat beside the sleeping child's bed. 'He really did love her, you know. But he could never have let her go.'

97

Alex's fingers enfolded hers.

'All that danger is over now, Lisa. You can forget your fears. Marc can't torment you any more.'

Tears brimmed her eyes.

'I did love him . . . right at the beginning . . . when I first met him. And Zoe was a result of the love I had for him. It was only later that everything started to go wrong . . . because of the drugs . . . '

"Then you must always remember the beginning, Lisa.'

He bent his head, resting it lightly against her brow.

'I'm not going to marry Fergus,' she said quietly.

His head lifted and his grey eyes stared at her, asking a question.

'You were right. It wouldn't be fair . . . to him . . . or to me. Marriage shouldn't be used as a shield, a defence, a protection. It has to be a sharing.'

Her voice lowered so that he could barely catch the words.

'And there must be love for that to happen.'

She gazed down at the glistening diamonds, then slowly slid the ring from her finger and placed it on the bedside table.

'You were right about so many things, Alex. Not every man is like Marc. But I have to learn to trust again . . . and I have to learn to love again.'

His mouth traced the outline of her closed eyelids, feathered softly down the curve of her cheeks, and paused at the corner of her parted lips while he murmured, 'I'll teach you.'

F3- RiG
fi fan.
WRl